Grassie

A Vanguard Origin

Written By:

R.D. Wolfe

Table of Contents

Chapter I – Temporary Fixes

The hum of trexium conduits rattled through the floor, too steady and too loud to ever fade into the background. Heat pressed down from the ceiling vents, heavy with the stink of oil and chemical coolant. The air always carried a faint metallic tang, the taste of ore dust that never seemed to wash out, not from your clothes, not from your skin, not from the back of your throat.

Grace lay wedged beneath the bulk of a processing valve, one boot braced against the frame, both hands buried in the guts of a machine that hadn't run right in three cycles. The casing was older than she was, its seams layered with weld scars and patch plates, each one proof that a "temporary fix" had been expected to last forever. Grease smeared across her knuckles, and a dark streak cut across her cheek where she'd brushed away sweat and forgotten about it.

"Hold it steady!" she barked, her voice muffled inside the metal cavity. Not sharp with panic, just the clipped tone of someone used to being ignored.

"I am holding it steady," came a muffled protest from the other side of the casing. The worker's gloved hands strained against the valve wheel, shoulders trembling with effort.

Grace rolled her eyes where no one could see. "Yeah? Then explain why it's trying to dance out of alignment." She shoved the wrench deeper into the seam, teeth gritting as the steel bit against her palm. The clang of metal on metal rang through the bay, drawing a few half-curious glances from others nearby but no offers of help.

Above her, the catwalk vibrated under heavy boots as someone passed. Nobody stopped. Grace was small enough to fit where the older techs couldn't, and young enough that no one minded letting her crawl into the cramped, blistering places.

The machine shuddered, coughed once, and then, impossibly, settled into a regular hum. The glow inside the conduit steadied, the pink light pulsing slow and even through the cracked seam.

For half a heartbeat, everyone froze. Silence in the refinery bay was worse than noise—ominous, like the world holding its breath.

Grace grinned into the darkness under the valve. "See? Fixed. All it needed was a couple well-placed threats."

From the catwalk above, someone groaned. "Or you broke it worse."

"What's worse than broken?" she shot back, sliding out from under the machine. "Either way, problem solved." She dusted her hands on her coat, leaving darker smudges behind. The smirk never left. "You're welcome."

A few of the engineers muttered, one or two even chuckled, but most had already drifted back to their slates and gauges. Grace always had a comeback, and she always made the work lighter, even when the hours stretched long and the heat pressed in. She didn't look like much—short, wiry, quicker than strong—but she fixed things others couldn't. She helped keep the refinery flowing, and that meant survival.

Even if nobody noticed.

Still, she was underestimated. She noticed it in every dismissive glance, every foreman who used her name like a punchline, every soldier who treated the engineers like furniture. Even the other laborers didn't give her much of a shot, always seeing them judge her before getting to see what she could do. She let them. Being underestimated meant you could get away with things others couldn't.

The machine coughed again. A low, stuttering sound ran through the pipe, followed by a sharp hiss. Pressure spiked.

"Back!" Grace shouted without thinking. She shoved the nearest worker away from the line and dropped her wrench. Her boots pounded against the grated floor as she sprinted three steps and slammed a manual bypass lever just as the seam split wide.

The pipe burst with a flash of pink light, trexium vapor hissing out like steam from a boiling kettle. Heat seared the air, blinding for half a second, coating the bay in a chemical haze that stung the back of the throat.

Men and women scrambled, some coughing, others swearing as they stumbled for cover. A handful ducked behind tool carts, one slipped and went sprawling, smacking an elbow hard against the floor. No alarms blared. None ever did in this bay. It was too common, too expected.

Grace, half-blinded and grinning anyway, laughed sharp against the chaos. "Relax! We're not dead this time."

When the vapor cleared and the bypass held, the hum steadied again, though higher pitched now, uneven. Grace stood bent over, hands braced on her knees, breath coming fast. Soot streaked her face, sweat cutting lines through the grime, but the grin didn't fade.

"Somebody better get me a ration bar," she said, straightening. "I just saved all your asses."

"Told ya!" came the voice from the catwalk, the same one that had heckled her earlier. "Broken worse."

Grace rolled her eyes but kept her mouth shut. The other engineers were already drifting back to their stations, some jotting notes on slates, others crouched by gauges that still quivered in the aftermath. The processor held... for now.

One of the older techs tapped the glass on a dial and gave a grunt. "Flow's back. But the bypass won't hold. Pressure's climbing in there, and this pipe's split clean through."

A ripple of curses passed through the men still in the area. Nobody wanted to be the one crawling ductside in the heat, not for a weld job that might last a day at best.

Grace leaned her shoulder against the wall, chewing the rest of a ration bar she'd stashed in her pocket earlier. She gnawed at it with the same enthusiasm she might've given cardboard. "At least it's moving again," she said around a mouthful. "Better cracked than cold."

That earned her nothing more than a snort. The older engineers spoke low, voices measured, already planning how to cut power long enough to weld. They didn't even glance her way.

Grace's eyes, though, stayed on the fracture line. From where she stood, she could see how the glow inside the pipe caught the faint edges of a spiderweb crack. It spread further than she'd thought at first — hairline fissures threading along the seam like veins.

She thought about pointing it out. She even opened her mouth once, but shut it again. The foreman would notice eventually. He always did.

She tossed the wrapper into a bin, wiped her hands on her coat, and muttered just loud enough to hear herself over the hum.

"Going to blow again before dawn if it's not sealed up quick."

Nobody looked her way.

By the time the gauges steadied and the others convinced themselves the bypass would last, Grace had already slipped away. Her ears still rang with the hiss of trexium vapor, and the sour stink of it clung to her clothes. She pulled the collar of her coat tighter as she walked, not because it helped with the smell, but because it made her feel like she was putting the refinery behind her.

The corridors outside were cooler, but only just. Layers of stone and steel pressed down from above, the ceiling low enough that taller men had to duck under the pipework that threaded overhead. Pink glow from the conduits pulsed along the walls, casting long shadows that shifted with each flicker of power.

Workers moved in steady streams—miners dragging themselves back from the shafts, engineers with grease still staining their hands, supply clerks hauling crates between storerooms. No one looked at her for long. Everyone had their own job, their own exhaustion.

Grace flexed her sore fingers as she walked. The skin along her knuckles was cracked from heat and grit, black with grease she wouldn't bother trying to wash off until lights-out. She could still feel the tremor of the pipe splitting under her hand, the way the glow had caught the spiderweb cracks no one else saw. The refinery would keep running tonight, but only because she'd been in the right spot at the right time. Nobody cared. Nobody ever did.

The smell shifted as she moved deeper into the stronghold. Chemical heat gave way to the earthy staleness of stored grain and root vegetables, then sharper notes of recycled protein drifting from the mess. Voices grew louder with each corridor, a rumble of laughter and complaints spilling into the narrow halls.

Her stomach tightened. It didn't matter how bad the food wasafter a shift in the bays, even sludge felt like a reward.

The mess was already buzzing by the time Grace slid through the line and onto the floor. Steam rolled off rows of metal trays filled with thick ration stew, the smell clinging to the air in a way that would outlast the meal itself. Long tables stretched wall to wall, every bench packed with workers hunched over bowls, their conversations blurring into a steady roar.

Grace wove through until she found the table where she usually sat. A cluster of mechanics and engineers filled it, most of them still in their work coats, streaked with grease or stone dust. She slid into an open spot, tray clattering down as she claimed her share of the noise.

Bow sat across from her, shoulders hunched over his stew like it might reveal its secrets if he stared long enough. His sleeves were rolled, skin marked by the faint scars of burns from too many hours on engine housings. He looked up once, gave her a quiet nod, and went back to poking at a slab of gray protein like he was deciding whether it was worth the effort to chew.

Dabs, by contrast, was in the middle of a story that drew half the table in whether they wanted it or not. His hands moved as fast as his mouth, waving wildly as he reenacted some disaster from the vehicle bays.

"I swear," he was saying, voice pitched too loud for comfort, "the crawler pitched sideways like a drunk goat, and the lieutenant—" he drew out the word with a dramatic sneer "—went face first into the mud. Helmet and all. Sounded like someone slapping a fish on a table."

A ripple of laughter ran around the table. One worker groaned, burying his face in his hands. Another muttered, "Dabs, shut up before someone overhears and makes you scrub latrines for a month."

Dabs grinned wide, unbothered. "Worth it. You ever seen a man of rank squeal when his boots fill up with swamp water? That image is going in my grave with me."

Grace shook her head, stabbing at her stew. "Grave's sooner if you keep talking that way."

Dabs caught her eye, smirk turning sharper. "Oh, look who's joined us. Grace the miracle worker. We heard you saved the refinery again today, didn't you? Got an old machine back on its feet?" He leaned in, elbows on the table. "You know, one of these days, one of those valve's going to blow and launch you clear through the ceiling. Pink streak across the barracks. Instant legend."

That earned him a few winces, but also chuckles. The guy next to him muttered, "You're sick," though he was grinning when he said it.

Grace rolled her eyes but couldn't fight the corner of her mouth twitching upward. "If that happens, I hope I land right on you. Take you out with me. Do everyone else a favor."

Bow huffed out something that might've been a laugh, quick and quiet, before going back to his food.

The conversation drifted to complaints about shortages, gossip about an officer reassigning a patrol crew, Dabs cracking another joke about the stew that was funny enough to make even the tired miners grin. Grace didn't have to lead the talk; she slid in when she wanted, her jabs sharp but well-aimed.

For once, she wasn't the overlooked kid in the ducts or the ignored voice in the bays. Here, in the mess with Bow's steady silence, Dabs' relentless noise, and the clatter of tired faces finding something to laugh about, she was just Grace—eating, laughing, belonging.

Chapter 2 – Days Off

A day off didn't mean the stronghold slowed down.

The refinery still thundered, the same as always, its hum rattling through the walls like a second pulse. Trexium ore came in by the ton, hot and unstable. Machines didn't care about shifts, and the stronghold was always hungry for more power. Someone was always watching the hoppers, patching pipes, or crawling ductside where the heat pressed in.

Grace's name had been scratched off the duty slate that morning with a quick mark of chalk. A day off, technically. The foreman would call it rest. What it really meant was the chance to catch up on all the things the last week hadn't allowed—patching clothes, bartering for parts, scrounging something better to eat than paste-thick stew.

The corridors were busier on days like this. Workers without shifts streamed through the narrow halls, their boots echoing against the mesh floors. A woman sat cross-legged near a vent, sewing a torn sleeve with bent wire. Two older men leaned over a pair of boots, arguing about whether the soles were worth saving. A boy not much older than Grace had spread a tray of scavenged hardware across a bench, little piles of hinges and screws lined neatly as if the order alone would make them valuable.

Grace drifted over, chewing the corner of a stale ration bar she'd pulled from her pocket. Her coat brushed her jaw, frayed fabric scratching her skin. She'd meant to mend it weeks ago. Another thing undone.

"How much for the clasp?" she asked, pointing with her chin at a brass piece the boy had set apart from the rest.

"Three-quarter ration," he said flatly. He didn't even look up.

Grace broke off half the bar with her teeth, dropped the piece into his hand, and pocketed the clasp. "Half's fair."

He shot her a look but didn't argue. Most didn't when food was the trade.

She kept moving, the press of the crowd tugging her deeper into the stronghold. The air shifted as she left the refinery halls behind—less chemical sting, more the sharp salt of soup boiling in the mess. Voices rose around her: laughter, bartering, the bark of a guard telling kids to clear the walk after they'd darted between benches. A cluster of men played cards with bent metal chits, cursing when hands went bad. Someone tuned a battered radio near the wall, coaxing out a few seconds of music before static swallowed it again.

Grace leaned briefly against the cool metal, closing her eyes. She could have gone back to her bunk. Could have slept through her free hours like everyone else always liked to. But she never wasted a day off on sleep. Not here. Not when there were scraps to trade, favors to call in, and friends to find.

Grace wandered deeper into the lower corridors, where the air lost the sharp edge of the refinery and settled into the faint damp of recycled water and metal left too long to cool. These halls were never meant for living. They were the spaces that happened in between—maintenance shafts, storage lanes, half-finished connector tunnels that became something else when the stronghold stayed in one place long enough for people to start bending the rules.

Someone had stretched canvas between support frames to make shade over a cluster of makeshift stalls. The fabric still bore the faded print of its old use—supply markings, half a coalition serial number—and it snapped lightly in the draft that slipped through the floor grating. Everything here could be torn down in a day if orders came: stalls folded flat, benches bolted into transport sleds, wiring unplugged from the conduit with practiced ease. But for now, it looked like a marketplace.

Grace slowed her pace, letting herself fall into the rhythm of it. Two miners traded a spool of copper wire for a set of patched gloves. Someone had rigged a hand-lamp to a trexium battery, its pink light swinging lazily as people passed beneath it. The smell of broth drifted from a drum perched over a portable heater—thin soup made from dehydrated roots, salt, and a hope that no one could quite name.

A vendor sold makeshift trinkets from a crate lid propped on two ammo boxes: bits of polished glass set into wire, a few colored threads braided into bracelets. Nothing anyone needed, everything someone wanted to believe could last longer than the walls around them. Grace lingered, fingering a scrap of cloth dyed an uneven yellow, the color of lightning streaking across the skies.

"Two meal credits," the vendor said, not looking up.

She snorted softly. "For half a rag?"

He shrugged. "Yellow's hard to find right now. Take it or leave it."

Grace dug into her pocket and flipped him a strip cut from a ration card. "Half credit. Better to sell it now than haul it to the next site."

He smiled at that, teeth white against the soot. "Deal."

She tied the strip of yellow fabric around her wrist, the knot uneven but tight enough. It wasn't pretty, but it was color, and color had a way of making even metal corridors feel human for a while. Plus, she liked how it made her think of lighting. Fast, powerful, and maybe a bit too noisy. Like her.

The crowd shifted around her—faces she half-recognized from the refinery or the mess, everyone half at rest but never still. Overhead, the conduits throbbed faintly with the power drawn from the mines below, a reminder that even the light over their heads was only borrowed from the next place.

Grace bought a small tin cup of steeped tea from a food stall whose heat coils hummed low under the counter; the liquid dark and faintly metallic from the water in this area. She carried it with her until she found an open crate and sat, the warmth seeping through her palms as she drank. The tea wasn't good—flat, iron-tasting—but it was hot, and that was enough. She watched a group of off-duty engineers unbolt a heater from the wall and drag it toward a transport cart, their laughter echoing through the narrow passage. The noise mixed with the hum of machinery, the rhythm of boots, the faint whistle of air vents. All of it was alive, but none of it was home. Except it was.

Days off were like that—quiet, restless, temporary. You pretended the stronghold belonged to you until the next move came, and then you packed your jokes, your makeshift comforts, your borrowed walls, and built them again somewhere else.

Grace took another sip and let her eyes wander up to the pink-lit conduit overhead, the pulse steady for now. Somewhere deeper in the structure, she could hear the refinery coughing through its next cycle, a reminder that nothing in the stronghold ever truly slept.

Grace lingered in the lower corridors until the air grew heavy with the scent of boiled roots and warm metal, the kind of smell that clung to the back of the throat. A faint tremor in the walls marked the start of another power draw—the stronghold adjusting itself, shifting weight and current to keep the balance right. The place was always doing that, flexing and breathing like something alive.

She rose and started back toward the mid-level walkways where the engineers kept their personal gear between moves. The space wasn't much—partitioned crates stacked into cubicles, narrow cots folded against the walls, and rows of lockers that could be unbolted and loaded onto transport sleds within an hour's notice. Every engineer learned to live with the same unspoken rule: nothing worth missing should be too heavy to carry.

Grace ducked into her corner space, brushing her hand along the tarp that served as a door. The air inside smelled faintly of oil and wool. A small heater hummed near the floor, its pink trexium core pulsing slow and even. She kept her tools sorted in metal tins, her clothes rolled tight and lined along the wall. On one shelf sat a scattering of things that didn't belong anywhere—old ration wrappers, a small carved token someone had traded her for a repair, the scrap of blue cloth from earlier tied around a nail like a flag.

She unrolled her blanket and sat on the cot, peeling her gloves off finger by finger. The fabric was stiff with grime, the leather splitting at the seams. She'd patch them later. For now, she just listened to the low hum of the heater and the sound of the stronghold shifting—bolts tightening, conduits sighing, the faint scrape of metal over metal that meant somewhere above, another section was being rewired for the next departure.

Nothing stayed still long. The walls she leaned against now might be part of someone's barracks two valleys over by next month. Even the floor under her feet would be stripped, stacked, and carted away when the move order came. The thought didn't bother her. She'd grown up inside that kind of impermanence. Stability was an illusion built by people who'd never had to pack their lives into a crate.

Still, she had her rituals. She reached for a tin of sealant and began rubbing it into the cracked leather of her gloves, small circular motions that filled the air with the sharp, clean scent of wax. It gave her hands something to do, a way to make the day last a little longer before she had to go back to the noise and heat.

The first sign that something was wrong came as a sound—a deep, hollow thud that shivered through the walls and left the air humming in its wake. Grace froze, one glove half way on, listening. A second thud followed, closer this time, and the heater's soft pulse flickered once and went dark.

She moved to the tarp and pulled it aside. The corridor lights stuttered, throwing sharp bursts of pink and shadow. Somewhere deeper toward the refinery, a siren wailed—short, clipped, then cut out entirely. The silence that followed was worse.

Dabs appeared at the end of the hall, breathless. "Pressure line blew near the storage conduits," he said. "Coolant's venting straight into the access bay. They're still inside."

Grace didn't stop to think. She grabbed a wrench from the pile of tools that had clattered to the floor in the rising wave of chaos and the insulated gloves hanging by the door. "Who's inside?"

"Two miners, one of the foreman's techs. Vent seals jammed."

They ran following Grace, who had clearly taken charge of the ensuing emergency. The heat thickened the farther they went; the air turning sharp with the stench of trexium coolant. By the time they reached the junction, fog was rolling along the floor in pale sheets, biting at their throats pink veins streaked through the vapor. Shapes moved inside—men shouting, silhouettes blurred in the haze. One was pounding on the manual release of the exit door.

Grace shoved past Dabs and ducked low under the vapor. "Don't breathe deep!" she yelled, voice muffled by her sleeve. "The coolant's eating the seals!"

The closest miner looked up, his mask smeared with condensation. "The lever's jammed!"

Grace knelt by the door mechanism; fingers already working at the emergency clamp. The metal burned cold against her gloves; the latch iced solid. She gritted her teeth and slammed the wrench into the hinge until the frost cracked. The next pull broke it free, the door jolting half open.

"Out! Move!" she shouted.

They stumbled through, coughing, their faces streaked with chemical frost. One of them slipped, catching his hand on a live wire. Grace yanked the line loose before it could arc, the spark snapping loud in the thin air. Someone behind her started to panic.

She turned on him sharply. "Hey! Eyes on me. You're breathing, right? Then you're fine."

That steadied them, just a little. Humor had a way of filling the cracks where fear tried to settle.

A tremor ran through the deck. The coolant tanks still inside the bay groaned under the pressure. Grace glanced at Dabs. "We need the emergency bypass now!"

He looked at her wide-eyed. "That's containment team work."

"Well," she said, grabbing the nearest tool pack, "guess they're short-staffed."

She dove into the service hatch, crawling toward the feed junction while the floor vibrated beneath her. The pressure gauge above her head was climbing fast, the needle flirting with the red. She found the bypass valve, twisted hard, then twisted again when it refused to move. Heat seared her palm even through the glove.

"Come on," she muttered. "Work with me."

A final shove broke the seal, and a rush of steam hissed through the pipes, venting the buildup away from the coolant tanks. The hiss evened out. The tremor stopped.

Grace backed out of the hatch, coughing, her hands shaking from the effort. The air was still sharp and heavy, but the worst of the coolant had cleared.

A figure stepped through the vapor, full Vanguard armor gleaming in the flickering light, the trexium glow tracing every curve of the plating and highlighting the deep, almost blood red streaks in the black of the armor. He moved with calm precision, like someone used to walking straight into chaos and expecting it to bend to his will without words.

"Clear the area," his voice rang through the mask, deep and even. "We've got the rest."

Grace hesitated, caught between shock and confusion. Grace stood, wiping coolant from her sleeve, meeting his gaze through the tinted visor. For a second, neither moved.

"Pressure's stable," she said, voice rough but steady. "System's venting."

He looked down at the gauge, then back at her. "Who authorized you to reroute?"

"No one," she said. "Figured paperwork could wait till after the explosion."

The faintest shift passed through his stance—a nod, maybe, or just surprise. "You could've killed yourself."

"Next time I'll try to schedule my near-death experience somewhere less noisy," she said dryly.

The Vanguard said nothing more. He turned away, issuing quick orders to the rescue crew now arriving with proper gear. But before he disappeared into the haze, he glanced back once, the light catching the faint scratches across his armor. A silent acknowledgment.

Dabs watched him go, then let out a low whistle. "You realize who that was?"

Grace exhaled, the adrenaline leaving her legs unsteady. "Nope. And don't particularly care at the moment."

Dabs laughed but let the moment lie. Grace looked up at him and took a deep breath.

"I need something to eat."

Chapter 3 — Authorizations

The story of the coolant bay still drifted through the stronghold, reshaped each time it changed hands. Nobody told it straight, but every version carried her name in it somewhere. Grace let it live on its own. Rumors kept people busy, and she'd long learned not to ruin good entertainment.

Work had taken on a different rhythm since then. Some shifts ended with a message clipped to her locker, scrawled in a precise hand she never saw write it: Request: G. Marrow. Authorization confirmed. No explanation. No name. The first time, she thought it was a mistake. The fifth, she'd stopped pretending to wonder.

The requests always came just as the stronghold started to quiet—when the generators settled into that slow, heavy heartbeat and the heat from the refinery dimmed. She'd pack her tools and follow the sound of the conduits, their hum faintly uneven where the current ran high. Sometimes she wound up crawling through vent shafts above the barracks, rerouting circuits while soldiers slept below. Other times it was the upper levels, sealed doors and armed guards posted outside pretending not to stare. The work never looked important, but the air around it always felt heavier than usual.

People noticed. Dabs more than anyone.

"You've been getting called off a lot," he said one night while they hunched over a stripped junction plate. "Same message, same handwriting. You fixing ghosts now?"

Grace pressed the wire against its clamp, sparks catching briefly along the edge of her glove. "If I am, they're paying better than the living."

Bow chuckled from where he was working near the vent. "You don't even tell the foreman anymore. He stopped asking."

"Safer that way," she said. "Less paperwork when something breaks."

Dabs shook his head, his grin fading into curiosity. "You come back different every time. Not bad, just... quieter. What's up there?"

Grace didn't answer. The hum under the floor seemed louder suddenly, the current pulsing steady as breath. "They don't like questions," she said at last, tightening another bolt. "And I like keeping my job."

It was half a lie, and they all knew it. The rules were simple— say nothing, ask nothing. The Vanguards who met her at those sealed doors didn't talk much either. They'd just nod once, step aside, and let her pass. Most wore full armor, faces hidden, voices filtered through static when they bothered to speak at all. Once or twice she thought she recognized him—the same Vanguard from the coolant bay—standing among them. His armor caught the light differently, edges dulled with use, the stance familiar even without the mask. He never said her name. He didn't need to.

The latest summons arrived during a meal break, a small metal slip slid beside her tray. She didn't have to open it to know what it said. Dabs caught the movement of her hand and frowned.

"Another favor?"

Grace pushed her tray away and stood. "Seems like it."

"Grace," Bow said quietly, "these favors—whatever they are— it's got a direction. Don't let it drag you where you don't want to go."

She smiled faintly, rolling her sleeves back. "If it starts pulling, I'll cut it loose."

The laugh they shared was thin, more habit than humor. She gathered her tools and left her friends sitting at the table. Outside, the corridors pulsed with low light, the hum of engines thrumming beneath her boots. The sound wasn't ominous anymore. It just felt expectant, like the stronghold itself had learned her pattern and was waiting to see where she'd go next.

Grace followed the sound before she saw the ship. The air on the upper decks always felt thinner, cleaner, and this time it carried the low pulse of engines being coaxed back to life. She traced it through a maintenance corridor that opened into the hangar—a temporary structure of scaffolding and cables, half dismantled from the last move and already being rebuilt around something new.

The airship hung there, massive and unfinished, the hull patched in sections of dull silver and dark alloy. Workers swarmed beneath it, voices muffled under the hum of equipment. The pink light from the trexium lines ran like veins through the floor, feeding into the vessel's core. It wasn't elegant, but it looked alive.

Grace stayed near the entry ramp, unsure if she was even meant to be here. Her orders had been thin as usual: *Maintenance support. Hangar Two.* She was still turning the slip over in her hands when a soldier stepped into her path.

"Area's locked down," he said. "Engineering clearance doesn't get you this high."

"Apparently it does today." She held out the order slip. The man scanned it, frowning at the code but saying nothing.

Another voice spoke from the catwalk above them. "She's cleared."

The soldier stepped aside immediately. Grace looked up. The man descending the stairs wore armor dulled from use, his helmet clipped at his side, the faint glow of trexium still pulsing along the seams. She recognized the shape of him before the face—the same Vanguard who'd walked out of the coolant bay haze without a word months ago.

He stopped a few paces away. "You're Marrow." His tone was even, not quite a question.

"Depends who's asking," she said.

He studied her for a moment, then nodded toward the ship. "One of the stabilizers is out of balance. Flight crew can't find the fault."

"I'm not licensed for airframes," she said, out of habit.

"Can you fix it?"

Grace hesitated, then nodded once. "Probably."

"Then you're authorized. Fix it." He started walking, expecting her to follow.

She caught up beside him, the deck vibrating under their boots as the engines cycled again. Up close, the armor looked old, edges burnished where color had worn away. He didn't talk much—most Vanguards didn't—but when he did, his voice carried that quiet kind of authority that didn't need to raise itself.

"How'd you know my name?" she asked finally.

He glanced at her. "You were hard to miss in the reports."

"Didn't realize saving your own skin got you reports."

"You know that's not what happened," he said, and left it there.

They reached the stabilizer array, a section of the ship's belly that hummed unevenly, the pulse irregular and sharp where it should have been smooth. Grace crouched beneath the housing, palms pressed to the metal, feeling the vibration climb through her bones. She ran through the checklist in her head—coolant flow, trexium regulators, the secondary dampers—each system flashing through memory as she listened for what didn't belong. The hum hitched at the same interval each cycle, too precise for a simple break. She muttered under her breath and reached for her toolkit.

The vanguard lingered a moment, then stepped away, his boots ringing across the deck as he joined the cluster of Vanguards near the wing struts. Their voices carried faintly through the hull, low and even. Grace tried to tune them out, but they threaded through the work no matter how she focused.

"Crosswinds'll tear us apart over the ridge if the current shifts again," one said.

"Too exposed," another replied. "If the raiders are still trailing the convoys, they'll see us before we clear the clouds. Plus, they've seen ferals in the area."

"Ferals?" One of them asked.

"Yeah, that's what soldiers started calling the infected who hang around, seem way more attracted to trexium cores than noise or movement like the others, you know. The ones who linger behind? They're less organized, but way more vicious."

She loosened a housing plate, counting seconds under her breath. The screw refused to move. She shifted her grip, nearly stripped it, hissed a curse she didn't bother to swallow.

"Regardless of what's there, you think they've got the power for that kind of chase?" the first voice asked again, closer now.

"They don't need it," came a third. "Not if they've got a ground crew feeding them trexium from the scavenged mines. We saw what they did to the western post."

Grace paused, the wrench hanging still in her hand. The words hit somewhere deep and cold. The western post had been a whisper, another rumor in a place full of them—storage fires, missing teams, an entire outpost swallowed by its own power grid. She'd never believed it. Not really.

The vanguard she had been talking to's voice cut through the others, quieter but certain. "We take the pass. Cargo stays sealed until we hit the eastern ridge. If the winds hold, we'll make it by dawn."

Someone asked what the cargo was. The silence that followed said enough.

Grace forced her focus back to the stabilizer. She moved through the rest of the checklist, recalibrating pressure valves, tracing conduits, her thoughts flicking between the systems and the voices above. It took longer than it should have—her attention snagged halfway through the diagnostics, replaying the word *cargo* in her head until she realized she'd skipped a step. She doubled back, found the fault hiding behind a cracked trexium regulator, and let out a quiet breath of relief.

She eased the replacement into place, the hum evening into rhythm. The deck shuddered under her palms, the vibration smoothing like a sigh. Around her, the Vanguards' conversation had turned to logistics—weather windows, escort timing, refueling at the eastern ridge. She kept her head down and her hands busy until the noise faded back into the steady heartbeat of the ship.

"Crosswinds'll tear us apart over the ridge if the current shifts again," one said. "We should cut wide through the lower valley."

"Too exposed," another replied. "If the raiders are still trailing the supply convoys, they'll see us before we clear the clouds."

The first voice snorted softly. "You think they've got the fuel for that kind of chase?"

"They don't need fuel," a third answered. "Not if they've got a ground crew feeding them trexium cores from the scavenged mines. We saw what they did to the western post."

Grace slowed her work, listening. She knew the place they were talking about—the western post had gone dark two weeks ago. Word was it burned from the inside, storage ruptures and chain fires so bright they could see them from the ridge.

"Orders stand," came another voice, deeper, quieter—the vanguard that she had been talking to. "We take the pass. Cargo stays sealed until we reach the eastern ridge. If the winds hold, we can make it by dawn."

Someone asked what the cargo was. The commander didn't answer.

Grace fitted the replacement part and sealed the housing, the hum smoothing back to a steady rhythm. The airship creaked slightly as the engines cycled, the entire hangar vibrating around her. Whatever mission they were preparing for, it wasn't routine freight; it was something heavier, something dangerous.

She checked the readings twice before sliding out from beneath the hull, the taste of oil and iron still sharp in her mouth. The noise of the hangar pressed back in—orders, shouts, the rush of hydraulics as the docking clamps released tension. Grace stood, wiped her hands on her coat, and looked up at the airship's massive frame. It thrummed steady now, the fault gone, ready to lift.

The vanguard who had given her assignment, broke away from the others when he saw her. He studied the display on a nearby console, then her. "You finished?"

"Stable current, balanced feeds. You're good to go," she said, flexing her sore fingers.

He gave a small nod, more acknowledgment than praise. "Impressive. The crews here spent 3 hours searching for what you fixed in 10 minutes. You'll be spending more time up here. My team's short a tech."

Grace frowned. "You've got your own engineers."

"Had," he corrected. "Our last one didn't make it back from the ridge run."

That landed like a quiet thud between them. Grace looked at the engine glow along the deck, the way it pulsed slow and even, like breath. "That supposed to make me feel better about saying yes?"

His tone stayed even. "No. Just honest."

She considered him a moment, then nodded. "Alright. I'll keep your ships running."

"Keep doing work like this, and you'll do more than that. Alright, I'll get your name submitted and assigned to our ground crew on temporary assignment. Nice work." He turned to go, but paused at the edge of the walkway when she called after him.

"You never said your name," she said.

He hesitated, then glanced back over his shoulder. "Varek," he said simply. "Leader of the War Born."

Grace repeated the name under her breath, and the sound of it caught in her chest. Everyone knew the War Born. They were the kind of Vanguard squad whispered about in mess halls and engine bays—the ones sent where the walls were falling and the lights had already gone out. The name carried a weight she could feel, more truth than title.

He was already halfway across the hangar again, issuing new orders. Grace watched him go, the hum of the engines echoing under her boots, the sound settling somewhere deep in her chest. Something about the way he said *temporary* made it feel anything but.

She gathered her tools and headed for the lift, grease still on her hands and questions she didn't have the nerve to ask turning over in her head. When the doors closed, the last thing she heard was the steady rhythm of the engines, like the stronghold itself had started a new heartbeat.

Chapter 4 — Manual Calibration

Grace lay flat beneath the hauler with her shoulders pressed to the cold metal deck, a half-dead work light trembling above her as the storm finally decided to commit. Rain rattled against the hangar's open doors in uneven bursts, the sound slipping in between the deeper noises of the stronghold—engines cycling, cranes whining, the distant thunder of the refinery still chewing through ore like it always did. The air was thick with the smell of burnt coolant, trexium exhaust, and damp metal, layered so heavily that it coated the back of her throat.

Someone above her was already cursing about the weather, the complaint echoing hollowly through the steel.

Grace ignored it.

The hauler's undercarriage was a snarl of weld seams and improvised wiring, some of it older than she was and retrofitted so many times that even the official schematics had stopped pretending to be accurate. Patch plates overlapped other patch plates, bolts mismatched and stripped, lines rerouted through spaces that had never been meant to carry current. It was the kind of machine that only kept running because enough people had refused to let it die.

Her tools lay arranged beside her in neat, deliberate rows, the only real order in the mess. She'd already replaced three of the four flow regulators, fingers still aching from forcing frozen couplings loose, and she was half convinced the last one had been welded shut on purpose by someone who'd hoped it would become the next shift's problem.

"Is it ready?" a voice called from somewhere above.

Grace braced one boot against the frame and leaned harder into the wrench without looking up. "Ready to collapse under its own weight, maybe."

A ripple of chuckles moved through the hangar, boots scuffing against the deck, the sound fading when another voice cut through it—steady, even, and familiar enough that her shoulders tightened a fraction before she let them drop again.

"Status, Marrow."

She rolled out from beneath the hauler, grease streaked up one arm and across her cheek, blinking against the brighter light as she pushed herself upright. Varek stood by the control station with his arms folded, armor dulled by rain and use, the red streaks along the plates darkened almost to black by the damp. A handful of War Born lingered behind him, quiet and watchful, the kind of still that suggested they were already thinking three steps ahead.

"Status?" Grace repeated, wiping her hands on a rag that had stopped being clean days ago. "Still alive. Barely. Same as this rig."

His brow lifted just enough to register the answer. "Meaning?"

"Meaning it'll run," she said, leaning back against the frame and crossing her arms, "but I wouldn't bet the trip on it. The regulator array's unstable, and the automatic calibrators are fried. Every time the core shifts, it throws the trexium flow out of balance."

One of the Vanguards behind him shifted his weight. "Can't we patch it and risk it?"

Grace snorted. "Sure. If you're fine losing power halfway through the valley and walking home in a storm. Unless your flyer friends feel like offering taxi service."

A low murmur rolled through the group. Varek didn't react.

"Options?"

"I can rig a manual calibration line," she said. "It'll keep the core balanced, but someone has to ride it while we're moving. The system's too unstable to trust automation."

He studied her for a moment, quiet enough that the hauler's hum seemed louder. "That someone would be you."

Grace hesitated just long enough to acknowledge that she'd already made the decision. "If you want it running, yeah. Otherwise, you're pushing."

The faintest twitch crossed his jaw, something like humor or resignation. "Then you're coming."

"That wasn't a request?"

"It wouldn't matter if it was." He turned toward his squad. "Gear up. We roll in an hour."

Grace exhaled, gathered her toolkit, and ducked back under the frame to tighten the last coupling until it bit clean. Thunder rolled low beyond the hangar walls, and the lights flickered once. Whatever waited out there was already moving closer.

The sky was a flat wash of gray when they rolled out, rain hissing against the crawler's hull as the storm settled into a steady drizzle. The vehicle groaned as it descended the ramp, joints rattling and panels shuddering, but it moved, and for now that was enough. There was only one crawler—Varek, the War Born, and roughly twenty soldiers packed inside. No convoy. No backup. Just steel, mud, and the quiet agreement that it would hold together long enough to matter.

Grace wedged herself between the control panel and a crate of spare parts, her toolkit strapped to the wall within reach. The air inside was heavy with damp metal and oil, the trexium hum vibrating up through the floor and into her ribs. She could feel every uneven pulse, steady for now, but close enough to unstable that she didn't let herself relax.

Varek stood near the forward hatch with one hand braced against the frame, watching the valley through the viewport. His armor caught what little light filtered in, blackened plates streaked red along the shoulders and sides.

"You paint those yourself?" Grace asked, nodding toward the markings as she adjusted the manual calibration.

He glanced back after a moment. "My little brother's favorite color," he said. "Thought red made things go faster."

She raised a brow. "Was he right?"

"He's dead," Varek said simply, turning back to the glass.

Grace swallowed the reply she'd been forming and focused on the console instead. "Good look anyway," she muttered, and if he smiled it was too faint to be sure.

Mist clung to the valley floor as they pushed deeper, trexium veins pulsing faint pink through exposed stone while soldiers settled into practiced quiet, checking straps and grips. Even the War Born watched the dark beyond the glass as if it was waiting to move. The power readings dipped, teasing the red, and Grace adjusted the calibration by feel, tapping the panel once as the hum steadied.

"Behave," she murmured.

A young soldier across from her smirked. "You always talk to machines?"

"Only the ones with personality."

The tension eased just a fraction.

Hours blurred together. Mud dragged at the wheels. Old relay towers slid past like ghosts in the fog. Once, the crawler lurched hard enough that a crate broke loose and had to be resecured, Grace barking instructions without raising her voice while rain hammered the hull and the trexium core throbbed a little too fast for comfort. The machine listened. It always did, eventually.

When the comm crackled with word that the relay tower was dark, Grace felt the tension tighten without anyone speaking. The crawler slowed as the storm thickened, the skeletal outline of the tower looming ahead with cables swaying and sparks jumping where trexium arced across broken joints.

"We move on foot from here," Varek said. "Grace, stay with the crawler. Keep the core balanced. I want it ready."

She nodded once. "Understood."

He lingered long enough to add, "Lock up when we're out," before the War Born vanished into the rain, swallowed by fog almost immediately.

Grace watched until the last armor light disappeared, then turned back to the console. The hum filled the silence, steady and strong for now.

The first impact came as a heavy thud against the hull, close enough to rattle her teeth. Grace snapped her eyes to the floodlight controls and threw them on, the world outside flaring white through the rain. Shapes moved low and fast toward the departing squad, skin slick and pale, eyes burning faint pink as they surged forward.

"Varek," she shouted into the receiver, already moving. "Ferals incoming—lots of them."

Another impact dented the hull inches from her head, tools clattering loose as the line bent under the sudden weight of bodies. Through the viewport she caught muzzle flashes in the mist as the War Born engaged, the line holding but bending under the press.

Grace glanced at the gauge and made the decision before fear had time to argue.

She stripped the safety fuses from the regulator lines, feeling the crawler protest as she whispered to it like a stubborn animal.

Residual momentum would carry it for a few seconds even without the core, and a few seconds was all she needed.

The crawler lurched forward as she threw it into drive, headlights tearing through rain and bodies as ferals scattered and then surged again. The hum climbed toward a shriek as she yanked the modular drive core free—already loosened from earlier adjustments—and wedged it between her knees while the machine began to slow. The casing hissed as she cracked it open, unstable pink light pulsing brighter with each second.

She leaned out through the open hatch, rain and grit slapping her face, and hurled the glowing core into the densest part of the swarm before using the crawler's last forward surge to throw herself clear.

The blast rolled through the valley like thunder made solid, light and heat flattening everything in its path as Grace hit the ground hard, mud and rain smearing across her face. When she forced her eyes open, the field was black and still, ferals scattered like broken things across the churned earth.

"Marrow," a voice said.

Varek stood nearby, armor scorched and red streaks dark with ash as he looked at her for a long moment. "You're out of your mind."

Grace managed a weak grin. "Seems to be working so far."

He shook his head, something like disbelief passing across his expression as he offered her a hand. "Next time, you warn me before you decide to blow something up."

She took it, fingers slick with rain and blood. "No promises."

Chapter 5 – Pending Confirmation

The refinery sounded the same when Grace came back.

Heat rolled out of the lower bays and met her in the stairwell, carrying the sour bite of coolant and the heavier smell of bodies that had been working too long. The hum under the floor was steady, the same layered vibration of pumps, conduits, and that one fan that always clicked twice before it spun up properly.

She stopped at the foreman's station long enough to press her thumb to the pad. His eyes stayed on the readouts.

"Grace," he said. "It says you were on a med hold. Did they clear you?"

"I'm here," she said.

He grunted, obviously apathetic to the situation. "Lines three and seven are drifting. Check seven first, but I need them both within spec today or we won't meet processing goals."

He didn't say anything else—no welcome back, no sideways joke, just giving her more work that needed doing.

Her locker stuck the way it always did. She hip-checked the dent near the handle and felt the latch give. Somebody had borrowed a rag and folded it wrong. Her coat hung where she left it. Gloves were shoved on the top shelf, still stiff from the last wash.

She pulled everything back into the order she liked without thinking about it. Coat first. Tool bag strap over her shoulder. Gloves last. The left one caught on the base of her thumb where the skin was still tight and shiny. She eased it on anyway.

Line seven sat in the same cramped run of corridor it had when she left, which felt like a full move ago. Low overhead. Warm wall on one side, hotter pipe on the other. The floor grate flexed under her weight.

Grace crouched by the regulator housing and ran her fingers along the bolts. One turned under her thumb more than it should have. She tightened it down, watched the gauge settle back into the range it was supposed to live in, and let her hand rest on the pipe long enough to feel the change in the vibration.

Her wrist complained when she pushed herself back up. The med tech had said it would do that for a while. She had decided not to care.

She was checking the gauge one more time when she heard the familiar clunk of bootsteps on the walkway behind her.

"You know you're allowed to take time off after blowing up a crawler," Dabs said.

Grace didn't turn around. "And leave you alone to repair things? I'd come back to a crater."

He came up beside her, coil of wire looped over one shoulder, hair still damp from a rushed wash. "Low chance. They stuck me on inventory yesterday. Counting bolts. I almost threw myself into the processor."

"Should've," she said. "Would've warmed the place up."

Dabs snorted. Some of the tension in his face eased. "You look rough."

"Crawl through a blast wave once," she said. "See how pretty you feel."

He leaned on the rail, watching her check the gauge again. "You could've just said you missed us."

"Missed you?" She moved to the next junction. "Best sleep I've had in years."

A quiet huff of air behind her might've been Bow. She glanced up in time to see him pass on the upper catwalk, a hand raised halfway in greeting before he dropped it to grip the line he was walking.

"Schedule's got you on three straight," Dabs said.

"I remember," she said. She checked the last connection on seven, found nothing new to fix, and straightened. "I'm fine, Dabs. Don't worry about me." She said, trying to sound confident in her tone.

Dabs didn't look convinced, but he let it go. "Mess at second bell?"

"If these things behave," she answered quipilly, nodding at the line she had just repaired as she made her way towards line three.

When second bell caught them mid work, she and Dabs were in the corridor watching a series of gauges and dials for the inevitable change that would mean something else needed to be tweaked. By the time they pushed through into the mess, the line was already snaking back toward the door. Same trays. Same smell of stew that always made her think of boiled socks. She took her usual seat. Bow sat opposite, quiet, tearing his bread into neat pieces before he ate them. Dabs dropped down beside her and immediately started a running commentary on the day's protein slab.

"This used to be something," he said, poking it with his spoon. "At some point in its life."

Dabs watched her for a second. "So you gonna tell us anything about what happened?" He asked, cheeking a mouthful of the bland meal. "There's tons of rumors."

"The food was better in the infirmary," she said.

He snorted. That was as close to an answer as either of them was going to get.

Nobody else at the table asked her what it had been like. The story was already out there doing laps without her help. She caught snippets from the next table over—"core went off like a flare," "ferals scattered," "Vanguard said"—but nobody pulled her into it.

That was fine. Work was simpler than explanations.

After the break she went back to the list. Line three did, in fact, decide it didn't want to live anymore. She coaxed the regulator back into place a second time, swapped out a sensor that had been lying about pressure, and only had to shut the line down once. She was proud about that.

By the time she turned in her slate, her arms ached in that old, familiar way from a day of fighting the same problems in the same corners of the bay. Her shirt stuck to her back. The bandage on her wrist itched under the glove.

She took the long way to the bunks. Past the storage bays. Past the lift that always caught on the second floor. The hum under the floor never changed. It filled the gaps where thoughts tried to creep in.

Her bunk was the same small space waiting for her. Thin mattress. Heater humming in the corner. The dent in the wall where she'd dropped a wrench months ago was still there.

Grace sat on the edge of the cot and tugged her boots off. For a minute she just sat like that, elbows on her knees, staring at nothing in particular while the noise of the stronghold settled into the background.

This was what life looked like. Pipes, heat, noise, Dabs talking too much, Bow not talking at all. After everything else, even that felt loud now.

The lights dimmed on third bell and the hum under the floor shifted with it, settling into the lower register Grace had come to associate with power being rerouted somewhere deeper in the stronghold. She lay back on the cot without bothering to pull her boots off, one arm tucked under her head, eyes fixed on the underside of the bunk above her where someone had carved a series of tally marks into the metal long before she'd claimed the space. They weren't evenly spaced, and whoever had made them hadn't bothered to keep count clean. A few lines overlapped. One had been scratched deeper than the rest, as if the person holding the tool had pressed harder on that one without quite meaning to.

She didn't try to figure out what they'd been counting. It wasn't her habit to wonder about other people's systems.

Her wrist throbbed when she flexed her fingers, the ache dull and persistent, the kind that didn't interfere so much as remind you it was there. She rolled it once and let her hand drop back to her stomach, the smell of oil still clinging to her coat despite the wash she'd given it earlier. Somewhere down the corridor a relay clicked, followed by the faint vibration of conduits adjusting load, and then the stronghold settled back into its usual rhythm of boots, voices, and the constant mechanical undercurrent that never fully went away.

She must have drifted off, because the knock caught her off guard. It wasn't loud, but it was deliberate, three measured taps against the frame that didn't belong to anyone she knew well enough to just push the tarp aside and lean in. Grace sat up, joints still stiff from the day, and pulled the tarp back.

Two Vanguards stood in the corridor. They weren't fully armored, helmets clipped at their sides, plating dulled and scratched in ways that spoke to use rather than neglect. One of them held a slate angled toward his chest. The color of the lights told her that she had more than drifted, it was almost time for her to get up anyway.

"Grace Marrow," he said, reading rather than asking.

She looked up from where she had been sitting and nodded once. "That's me."

"You're being reassigned," he said, shifting the slate in his hand so she could see it without stepping closer. Her name was already there, ident code routed through a channel she didn't recognize.

"Reassigned where?" she asked, pushing herself to her feet and brushing dust from her hands as she spoke.

"Vanguard support."

Grace took a second longer than usual before responding, eyes on the slate. "For how long?"

The two Vanguards exchanged a glance, brief and unremarkable, the kind that didn't invite comment.

"Depends," one of them said. "On need."

She nodded again, as if filing it with the rest of the day's instructions, and glanced back toward her bunk. "So I'm still engineering."

"Yes."

"Just not refinery."

"That's right."

She let out a short breath and turned back into the space. The bag came first, strap settling across her shoulder as it always did. She opened it long enough to check the contents, fingers moving through familiar order while the Vanguards waited where they were. Tools. Spares. Gloves shoved into the outer pocket. Everything accounted for. She paused at the shelf, fingers brushing the scrap of cloth tied to the nail, then left it where it was and turned back toward the corridor.

They fell into step without comment, Grace between them, their pace steady and unhurried. Doors along the corridor opened as they approached and closed again behind them. Guards glanced up, eyes tracking the armor before briefly settling on her, then returned to their stations. The hum under the floor stayed the same, vibrating up through her boots as they moved farther from the refinery levels.

"This temporary?" she asked after a few turns, adjusting the strap of her bag when it slipped against her shoulder. "Or temporary-temporary?"

One of them answered without looking at her. "You'll be told if it changes."

She nodded. "Alright."

They stopped at a lift she didn't recognize. One of the Vanguards keyed it and stepped inside. Grace followed, turning to face the doors as they slid shut. The lift dropped smoothly, vibration steady enough that she leaned back against the wall without thinking about it.

"Do I need new clearance?" she asked, rolling her wrist once when it twinged.

"You'll be issued what you need."

"Simple enough, I guess," she said.

The lift slowed and opened onto a brighter level. The air was cooler here, sharper, the smell of coolant and ozone replacing the heavier refinery heat. Wiring ran clean along the walls, labeled instead of patched. People moved through the space without slowing, slates in hand, stepping around one another with practiced ease.

Someone was waiting just beyond the doors, already reading from a slate. They glanced up when Grace stepped out, eyes flicking from her face to the ident code on the display, then back down again.

"You weren't scheduled," they said, thumb pausing over the screen.

Grace shifted the strap of her bag higher on her shoulder. "That tracks."

The person frowned and scrolled back through the entry, lips moving slightly as they checked the routing. "Support assignments don't just—" They stopped and looked past her at the two Vanguards. "There's no record of a transfer window."

"She's with us," one of the Vanguards said. His voice was even, already finished with the conversation.

The person hesitated. "I still need authorization logged. Otherwise this throws off—"

The Vanguard didn't respond. He just looked at the man. It wasn't aggressive. He didn't step closer or raise his voice. He stood where he was, armor still, hands relaxed at his sides, waiting. Silently.

The silence stretched. A few people passed behind them without slowing. The hum of the systems filled the space between breaths.

The person glanced back at the slate, then at Grace, then finally dropped their eyes and sighed through their nose. "Fine," they muttered, fingers moving quickly now. "Temporary intake. Flagged pending confirmation."

"Mark it down," the other Vanguard said.

"It's marked it's marked," they replied, a little sharper than before. Then they stepped aside and turned down the corridor. "Come on."

Grace followed, adjusting her bag again as she walked. Behind her, the lift doors slid shut, and the sound of the lower levels folded back into the stronghold, the hum underfoot steady and unchanged, even here, or maybe that was just her imagination.

Chapter 6 — Sequences

The training bay had been built for repetition. Benches ran in straight rows, each one fitted with the same brackets and tethers, the same sealed kits waiting to be opened and closed again. Slates sat at the corner of every station like quiet judges, logging sequence and time with no interest in whether the hands in front of them were tired or irritated or familiar with better ways to get the same result.

Grace stood at her bench with her sleeves rolled back and her fingertips resting on the metal edge while the overseer recited the sequence. He spoke without urgency, the words practiced and flat, the same cadence he gave everyone no matter what they'd done before they arrived here. Disassemble. Inspect. Reassemble. Certify. There was always an extra pause around the parts that mattered to them, as if pausing made obedience easier.

The module assigned to her station was a Vanguard interface core, heavy and clean, sealed tighter than anything she'd ever been allowed to open in the refinery. The housing had no weld scars, no patch plates, no improvisation baked into it. It looked like a thing that had been designed to behave.

She released the clamps and lifted the cover free, setting it aside without aligning it to the marks. Her hands went to the interior the way they always did, pulling components in the order that made sense to her instead of the order that sat on the slate. Regulation came out clean. Transfer followed. When she reached the feedback assembly, she slowed and turned the ring once under her fingers, feeling the faint unevenness that wouldn't show on a gauge until later. Her thumb hovered over the adjustment point, ready to make a small correction that would keep it from returning.

The checklist sat open on the slate beside her. The step she wanted to do next wasn't next on the list. Grace set the ring back in place anyway and moved on.

She finished reassembly quickly, quicker than most of the trainees around her, and slid the unit into the testing cradle. The diagnostics began their crawl across the slate, bars filling at a pace that never matched the speed of her hands. The overseer drifted behind her bench and stayed there, close enough that she could feel him watching the log while she waited. Grace kept her palms flat on the bench, fingers splayed, staring at the bare metal in front of her as the seconds dragged out.

The slate finally chimed. A bright chip of green flashed across the display—approval, clean and final.

Grace didn't look up. She let the sound wash over her, let the success sit where it was without giving anyone the satisfaction of seeing it on her face.

"You skipped ahead," the overseer said, tapping the slate once as if the log offended him more than the outcome ever could.

"The checks cleared," Grace replied, still facing the bench, trying to keep the weeks of procedural frustration out of her voice.

"They did," he said, a note of derision entering his voice as it did for most of the people in this new phase of her life. "The sequence didn't."

She nodded once and began resetting her station, clearing the kit and aligning the next set of components the way the manual wanted, not the way her hands wanted. The overseer marked something on his slate and moved down the line without another word.

On the next cycle she stayed inside their order. Same core. Same internal layout. Same feedback assembly waiting in the same place. Her hands moved slower this time, not because she didn't know what she was doing, but because she was making herself walk the steps the way the slate wanted them walked. When she reached the feedback ring, she left it alone and kept going, watching the checklist as if it might change its mind.

The unit passed inspection again. The slate chimed its approval, and a moment later a brief fluctuation flickered across the diagnostics before settling back into tolerance.

Two benches down, a trainee fought with a connector that wouldn't seat, forcing it until the housing flexed. Grace glanced over, saw the angle was wrong, saw the tension point in the bracket. She returned her eyes on her own bench anyway. The overseer stepped in, corrected it by the book, and stood there until the trainee repeated the step exactly the way it was written. When the connector finally slid home, the slate chimed, and the overseer moved on as if nothing had happened.

Assignments posted for the next module. Names scrolled on a slate near the front of the bay. Grace wiped her hands on a rag that didn't need it and walked over with the others. Her name wasn't there. She read the list twice, then stepped back without comment and returned to her bench. No one looked at her long enough to give her anything to respond to.

She was midway through another disassembly when she became aware of someone standing at the end of her station. The presence was familiar before the face was. Varek watched her hands instead of the slate, armor dull in the bright light, posture still.

"You're ahead," he said, quiet enough that it wasn't meant for anyone else.

Grace kept her eyes on her fingers moving over the small components. "It's not hard."

He stood there while she worked through the prescribed sequence, saw the moment her hand slowed at the feedback assembly, saw her leave it untouched and move on. When she seated the unit in the cradle, the overseer drifted back again, eyes on the diagnostics, smirking as if the delay proved something.

The second moved like it was thick. The slate chimed. Another flash of green. Grace kept her gaze down, still trying to keep her annoyance at this level of specificity to a minimum. Varek hadn't moved.

"You'll get faster," he said after a moment, his voice pitched low enough that it didn't carry beyond the bench. It wasn't encouragement. It sounded more like a placeholder, something said because silence eventually invites questions.

She slid the components back into alignment, tightened the clamps, and logged the reset before answering. "I'm already fast."

"I meant at slowing down."

That earned him a brief glance from her. She went back to the kit. "Seems like a strange thing to train for."

He shifted his weight slightly, the faint sound of armor moving under the lights. "It keeps things uniform."

"Uniform's not the same as stable," she said, still focused on the bench.

"No," he agreed. "But it's easier to replace."

Grace exhaled through her nose and reached for the next component. The words sat there between them, not quite accusation, not quite agreement. She didn't bother responding right away. The sequence demanded her attention again, and she gave it what it wanted, step by step, resisting the small corrections that kept presenting themselves as she worked.

After a few moments she said, "They don't like that I don't do it their way."

"They don't like that you have a different way," Varek said. "Those are different problems."

She paused, hands still, then resumed without comment.

"They see refinery work as reactionary," he continued, watching her fingers instead of her face. "Fix it when it breaks. Patch it when it fails. Keep it running at any cost."

"And this is better?" she asked.

"This is controlled," he said. "Which, when you're being shot at and need to pick up where someone else left off, has its value."

Grace seated the module and waited for the slate to catch up, eyes on the bench again as the diagnostics ran their course. The pause stretched, familiar now, irritating in a way that felt increasingly intentional.

"So why keep me here," she asked, "if I don't fit the system?"

Varek didn't answer immediately. He waited until the slate chimed and the green flashed again before speaking. "Because having someone who can solve a problem regardless of the circumstances or the order of things is valuable. Things don't always break where people train for them to. It's usually somewhere far more inconsiderate."

She nodded once, absorbing that without looking at him.

"And when they do," he added, "the people who follow the sequence perfectly are usually still waiting for permission to fix it. That puts people like me in a dangerous position when we need things to just... work."

Grace reset the bench one more time, slower now, more deliberate, letting the routine carry her through the last steps. Before locking the housing, she made the same small adjustment she'd made before, logged and documented in the narrow margin where compliance and necessity overlapped.

The slate accepted it again.

Varek watched that too, said nothing about it, and finally stepped back. "You won't be popular here," he said, as if noting the weather.

She almost smiled. Almost. "I'm getting the impression I wasn't brought here for that."

"No," he said. "You weren't."

He left her there with the bench and the next kit already waiting. Grace stood for a moment longer, hands resting against the metal, listening to the steady, indifferent rhythm of the bay. Then she picked up the tools again and started the sequence over, doing it their way where she had to, and her way where it counted, even if no one else noticed yet.

The training went on over weeks of procedure that grated against Grace's sensibilities. She was tired of doing things in order over and over, logging what step she did first, second, third. She did it anyway. Finally, blessedly, after nearly a month of procedure memorization, she was done and got to move on to actually fixing things, and not just proving that she could fix them in the right order.

Grace stood half inside a flight crew compartment with her shoulders wedged between the frame and a rack of avionics, one knee braced against the seat to keep herself steady while the ship idled. The HUD assembly lay open in front of her, its housing split cleanly, layers of projection hardware exposed and humming softly. She'd been asked to recalibrate drift and latency, nothing dramatic, just enough of an adjustment that the overlay would stop lagging behind the pilot's movements when the ship banked hard.

She worked slowly, deliberately, the way she'd learned to here. Not because she needed to, but because rushing drew attention she didn't want. The pilot sat a few feet away, helmet off, watching the deck crew move through their preflight checks with the kind of focus that suggested muscle memory had taken over hours ago.

"Any luck?" he asked, glancing at the transparent panel hovering in front of him.

Grace tightened the last fastener and slid back enough to see the display from his angle. "Give it a second," she said. "It'll catch up."

The projection flickered once, then stabilized, horizon line settling where it was supposed to be. The pilot rolled his shoulders and nodded in relief. "That's it."

She smiled, logged the adjustment, and sealed the housing, fingers already moving toward the next task when the hangar shifted around them. Voices dropped. Movement changed direction. The kind of quiet that didn't come from discipline so much as anticipation.

Grace straightened and leaned back against the bulkhead, wiping her hands on a rag that was already stained beyond saving. She didn't need to ask what was happening. You learned the difference between routine and response quickly in a place like this.

Varek crossed the hangar floor, armor sealed, helmet clipped at his side. He was flanked by two Vanguards she didn't recognize and a third figure moving just behind them, taller, broader, carrying himself with the easy weight of someone who had spent a long time being expected to survive. Achilles, she realized distantly, filing the name away because she'd heard it enough times to recognize the silhouette.

They weren't War Born. Not all of them. Grace noted it without knowing why it mattered.

Varek stopped near the flight crew bay and took a call, turning slightly away from the noise. Grace went back to her slate, pretending to review the HUD calibration while listening anyway. You didn't survive long in support if you didn't learn how to hear without looking like you were listening.

"Yes," Varek said. A pause. "Understood." Another. "We'll handle retrieval."

He ended the call and turned back toward the hangar. That was when he finally looked at her.

"You're done here," he said.

Grace blinked once. It wasn't a question.

"Grab your kit."

She didn't ask why. She closed the panel, clipped her tools back into place, and followed him toward the transport that was already being prepped at the far end of the deck. The pilot she'd been working with watched them go, expression unreadable.

They boarded quickly. No briefing. No destination given. Grace strapped herself into a side seat and secured her kit beneath her feet as the engines spun up. Across from her, Achilles checked his weapon with practiced ease, movements economical, almost bored. The others did the same, quiet in a way that suggested this wasn't their first deviation from plan.

The flight was rougher than usual. Grace felt it in the way the hull vibrated, in the way the pilot adjusted course more often than he should have needed to. She kept her eyes on the diagnostics scrolling across the small auxiliary display, watching numbers settle and spike and settle again.

They touched down hard, the impact shuddering through the frame and rattling the kit beneath Grace's boots. The engines didn't spool down all the way, holding at a low, uneven idle that carried through the deck in a way she didn't like. She stayed strapped in as the ramp cycled, listening to the change in sound as air and heat pushed briefly into the cabin before sealing again. No one moved toward the exit. Whatever was happening outside, it wasn't the part she was needed for.

Varek stood first and stepped off the transport followed by the rest of the makeshift Vanguard team, the ramp sealing behind them before anyone else followed. Grace watched the diagnostics instead, eyes tracing the same loops twice while the others waited in practiced stillness.

Time stretched in an unnatural way. Grace found herself counting the rise and fall of the engine hum, noting the slight delay between cycles. When the ramp finally opened again, it did so with less urgency, the outside noise muted, the air carrying a sharp, scorched tang that clung even after the hatch sealed once more.

Varek returned first. Behind him came another Vanguard in older armor, the finish worn dull from use. Between them walked a figure who wasn't Vanguard at all, at least not yet. Grace noticed the armor immediately—training issue, smaller frame, plates warped and blackened where they'd taken hits they hadn't been built to absorb. Power routing lay exposed along one side, manually bypassed and still warm enough to register faintly on Grace's slate as the figure passed.

They guided her toward the rear of the cabin and seated her near the bulkhead, movements careful without being gentle. The girl followed the direction without resistance, posture rigid, steps measured as if she were still waiting for the next command to come from somewhere else. Her helmet was placed at her feet and squared neatly against the deck. Her hands rested in her lap, fingers slack but not loose, eyes fixed on the space between her boots. Two others, with similarly haunted expression took their places in the back of the airship.

Grace stayed where she was and opened her slate, logging what she could without touching anything. The armor told its own story if you knew how to read it—stress fractures that hadn't yet propagated, heat scoring where systems had been forced to carry load past tolerance, stabilizers that should have failed and didn't. This wasn't doctrine holding. This was someone refusing to stop moving.

Varek removed his helmet and sat across from the girl, leaning forward slightly as he spoke. Grace couldn't hear the words over the engines still cycling, but the cadence was even, unhurried, the same tone he used when he wasn't asking for anything back. The girl didn't respond. She shifted once when the flier adjusted position, shoulders tightening before settling again, gaze never lifting from the deck.

After a while, Varek stood and turned toward the rear hatch. "I'll be back," he said, not loudly, not to anyone in particular. He glanced toward Achilles, who rose without comment and crossed the cabin to sit beside the girl, close enough to be present without crowding her. Varek stepped through the hatch and sealed it behind him.

The flier lifted again, smoother this time. Grace kept working, noting where the armor would need to be powered down before anything else could be touched, where the routing would have to be rebuilt instead of patched. Achilles spoke quietly beside the girl, his voice low and steady, questions spaced out, answers coming slower and not always in full sentences. A name surfaced once, then another, spoken softly and left alone. Grace didn't write those down.

When Varek returned, he didn't sit. He stood near the hatch while it was still cycling closed, one hand braced against the frame, looking out over the land slipping beneath them. Grace glanced up at the reflection in the reinforced glass and caught them both there at once—the girl seated near the rear, shoulders drawn in, eyes still down, and Varek at the edge of the ship, squared to the horizon, unmoving.

The image held just long enough to register before the seal locked and the reflection fractured.

Grace lowered her gaze back to the slate and finished the report she could finish. The rest would wait until the armor came off, until someone else decided what happened next. For now, all she needed to know was that the systems had held longer than they should have, and that whoever was inside them hadn't been given time to stop yet.

She closed the slate and secured her kit as the flier turned back toward the stronghold, the engines settling into a steadier rhythm.

Whatever this mission had started as, it hadn't ended as training.

Chapter 7 – The Courtyard

Grace had learned that if you wanted to get somewhere quickly, you took the straight corridors and ignored everyone calling your name, but if you wanted to know what mood the stronghold was in, you took the longer routes and paid attention to who tried to stop you.

The maintenance bay outside Hangar Three was loud enough to qualify as a social gathering, which told her most of what she needed to know before she even stepped fully inside. Equipment crates had been pulled out of their neat rows and stacked wherever there was room, toolkits sat open on the deck like someone had meant to come back to them in a minute and never quite had, and conversations carried in overlapping layers that rose and fell with the pitch of the engines cycling overhead. It smelled like oil and warm metal and the faint tang of coolant that never really washed out of a place once it settled in, and the floor plates under her boots rattled just enough to remind her that the stronghold was still borrowing time from the valley whether it admitted it or not.

She made it three steps in before someone called her name, the shout half-lost in the noise and half-amused, as if the person had been taking bets on how long it would take her to show up.

"Marrow—hey, Marrow!"

Grace didn't stop right away, letting the call bounce once more off the low ceiling while she adjusted the strap of her toolkit and stepped around a pallet of stripped weapon housings, then slowed just enough that the person calling could catch up without having to jog. When she finally turned, one eyebrow already lifted, the tech skidded to a halt in front of her, breathless and grinning in a way that suggested he'd been sent rather than inspired.

"If this is about the coupling in Bay Four," she said, glancing past him toward the work benches, "it's not haunted, and hitting it harder isn't going to change its mind."

The tech laughed and waved a hand, still catching his breath. "Not mine. I wouldn't bother you over that. War Born put in a request."

Grace sighed and rolled her shoulder, the sound long-suffering enough to be convincing without being entirely sincere. "Of course they did."

"They always do," he said, and this time there was no grin in it, just the quiet acknowledgment of a pattern they'd both seen enough times to stop pretending it was temporary.

She followed him the rest of the way into the bay, weaving between racks of half-disassembled equipment and skirting a knot of engineers arguing over a diagnostic slate that kept insisting everything was fine when it very clearly wasn't. The hum of the hangar settled into her bones as she walked, the vibration familiar enough that she could tell when something was off without looking at a readout, and she noticed the way people's eyes tracked her movement even when their conversations didn't pause, the small recalibrations that happened when someone assumed help might actually arrive.

Two Vanguard support engineers stood near the central bench, both of them mid-argument until they spotted her, at which point one of them broke off with a short laugh and gestured in her direction.

"There she is," he said. "I told you she'd show."

"I told you she'd be annoyed about it," the other replied, folding her arms and studying Grace with an expression that suggested she'd already resigned herself to being right about that too.

Grace dropped her toolkit onto the bench and leaned over it, popping open a weapon housing without ceremony while the metal was still warm. "You two arguing over who gets to explain this to me," she said, "or are we skipping to the part where something's not doing what it promised?"

The woman snorted, the sound sharp but not unkind. "Nothing's broken. Yet."

"Which is usually worse," Grace said, fingers already moving as she traced a connector path and twisted a component free to inspect the contact points. The hum inside the housing smoothed slightly under her hand, and she replaced the piece without comment, tightening it just enough to feel the resistance settle where it belonged.

The man shifted his weight and cleared his throat. "War Born's rolling out later. They want you on standby."

Grace didn't look up. "Standby for what."

He hesitated, then shrugged. "Whatever decides to misbehave."

She huffed quietly, the corner of her mouth lifting despite herself. "You know that's not an answer. They're going out on assignment. We don't usually have the honor of tagging along unless something's broken. So what's broken and who broke it?"

The woman leaned back against the bench, watching Grace's hands more than her face. "Transport rig's throwing faults that don't stick," she said. "Auxiliary systems feel like they're pulling uneven, but the numbers keep smoothing out before anything trips. We thought it was the grid."

Grace didn't answer right away. She pressed the housing panel back into place and rested her palm against it, feeling the vibration through the metal instead of watching the slate, because trexium had a habit of behaving politely right up until it didn't. "It's not the rig," she said finally. "At least not by itself."

Both of them looked at her.

"They're hauling recovered trexium," Grace continued, glancing toward the hangar doors where the War Born transport waited, half-loaded and impatient. "Unrefined. Still volatile. That much unstable material needs a stabilizing unit just to keep it from shaking everything else apart, and if they've tied that unit into auxiliary power instead of isolating it, the whole system's going to feel wrong without ever admitting it." She lifted her hand from the panel and wiped it on her coat. "Which means the readings stay clean right up until something draws harder than expected."

The woman let out a slow breath. "So nothing's broken."

Grace shrugged. "Nothing that wants to admit it."

They exchanged a look, this one heavier than the last, and Grace straightened, already reaching for her toolkit. "Their assignment's coming up," she said. "If they're going after a trexium stash, someone needs to babysit that stabilizer the whole way. If it slips, it won't just take the hub with it."

That earned her another glance, this one confirming what they'd been trying not to say.

She slung the toolkit back over her shoulder and turned toward the hangar doors. "Alright. I'll take a look. But you owe me."

One of them hesitated, then smiled faintly. "What do you want?"

Grace looked back over her shoulder as she walked. "You know what I want."

"Food!" they shouted in unison.

"Damn right," she called back.

As she stepped into the wider hangar, the noise opened up around her, engines cycling and loaders shouting over one another as equipment was moved into place with the kind of practiced urgency that came from knowing how quickly things could go sideways if you let them. War Born's transport sat near the far end, scarred and utilitarian, surrounded by techs who were trying very hard not to look relieved when they saw her heading their way.

The engines spooled higher as the hangar noise fell away behind sealed bulkheads, the transport shuddering once as clamps released and the deck tilted just enough for Grace to feel the change in her knees before the vibration settled into a new pattern. The hum was deeper now, less forgiving, power moving with intent instead of idling politeness, and she braced one hand against the interior frame as the airship cleared the bay and committed itself to the climb.

War Born moved through the interior without comment, harnesses clipped, weapons stowed but close, their presence registering more as weight than motion. Grace kept to the systems bay near the midline, toolkit already open at her feet, slate clipped magnetically to the bulkhead where she could see it without craning her neck. The auxiliary feed spiked as they banked, just enough to confirm what she'd already known from the hangar, and she adjusted the temporary routing by feel, thumb and forefinger tightening a regulator that responded a half-second slower than it should have.

"Don't like that," she muttered, not to anyone in particular, and felt the vibration smooth in response, the airship's pulse evening out as if it had decided to cooperate for the moment.

One of the War Born hovered nearby, close enough to be useful without getting in her way, his eyes flicking between her hands and the readouts with the kind of focus that came from knowing exactly how much trouble a bad number could cause at altitude. "It was fine on the ground," he said.

"It usually is," Grace replied, shifting her weight as the deck angled again and the power draw surged to compensate. "Ground doesn't ask much."

She leaned in farther, forearm pressed against warm housing, tracing the feed line as it disappeared into a nest of older components that had been retrofitted twice and documented once, the wiring carrying the faint discoloration of heat stress that never quite made it into official reports. The stabilizing unit wasn't failing so much as it was being asked to pretend it wasn't tired, and it had gotten very good at pretending.

The airship leveled out, engines settling into a steady climb, and Grace felt the momentary lull in strain as clearly as a held breath finally released. She took advantage of it, swapping a limiter she'd flagged earlier and reseating the connection with a fraction more resistance than spec called for, trusting her hands over the manual in a way that had kept her alive long enough to know when to push.

Behind her, boots shifted as someone moved closer, and she caught the reflection of armor in the polished edge of the panel without turning her head. Varek's voice came from just over her shoulder, low and even, pitched to carry through the engine noise without competing with it.

"How long will it hold?"

Grace tightened the last fastener and leaned back on her heels, eyes on the readout as it recalibrated into something closer to honest. "Long enough to get us there," she said. "Longer if we're gentle. Shorter if we're not."

"That's not an answer."

She glanced up at him, one corner of her mouth lifting. "It's the best one I've got."

The transport lurched as it caught a crosscurrent, engines compensating hard enough that the hum climbed into a register Grace didn't like, and she reached out without looking to steady the panel, fingers already adjusting the feed to bleed off the worst of the spike before it could cascade.

"Try not to throw us around too much," she added, eyes back on her work. "This thing's temperamental."

Varek didn't respond, but a moment later the movement smoothed, the airship's course adjusting in a way that suggested her message had been received without argument.

Grace exhaled slowly and went back to the system, hands moving faster now, momentum carrying her along as the transport cut through the sky toward whatever waited ahead, the problems already stacking up in her head in the order she'd deal with them when they arrived. For now, the numbers held, the vibration stayed within tolerances she could live with, and the airship continued forward under her care, systems bending just enough to keep pace without breaking.

They touched down in the middle of what had once been a courtyard; the skids grinding against fractured stone and half-buried metal as the transport settled into a space that had been designed for ceremony and traffic and now existed only as a bowl of broken angles and exposed sightlines. The ramp dropped into quiet that felt wrong for a fallen stronghold, the kind of stillness that came from things already having moved out of the way, and War Born flowed off the transport with practiced confidence, fanning out toward the interior passages that led deeper into the structure where the trexium cache was supposed to be waiting.

Grace stayed behind with the crate.

It squatted in the center of the courtyard, reinforced plating and hazard markings, its stabilizers humming steadily as she checked the readouts and made small adjustments to keep the unrefined trexium inside from reacting to the uneven ground and the echoes of movement around it. The crate wasn't dangerous yet, not on its own, but it was sensitive to everything, and Grace had learned the hard way that "not yet" was the most expensive phrase in engineering.

The first shots came from the passage War Born had just disappeared into, sharp and close enough that the sound snapped back into the courtyard before the echoes could stretch out and die.

Grace looked up from the crate just in time to see movement flicker at the far edge of the opening, shapes resolving into people where no one had expected any, and the quiet shattered as return fire answered from multiple angles at once.

Raiders.

Not a patrol, not a probing force, but a group already inside and waiting, their timing too good to be coincidence as they surged toward the same prize War Born had come for. Grace felt the crate react immediately, the stabilizers tightening as vibration from the first exchange rippled through the courtyard, and she dropped lower beside it, hands steady as she compensated and watched the glow inside the crate brighten and dim in quick, irritated pulses.

War Born fell back fast, not routed but forced, the ambush collapsing their advance and driving them out of the passages and back into the open bowl of the courtyard where cover was sparse and angles were bad. Raiders pressed hard, numbers filling the openings and spilling into elevated positions that had been invisible seconds earlier, and Grace understood the shape of it almost before she understood the danger, the geometry of the space snapping into place in her head with the same clarity as a schematic.

They were losing ground. They were going to keep losing it. If the fight stayed here much longer, the crate was going to become a liability instead of an asset.

Grace's eyes flicked to the transport behind her, to the open bay where fallback equipment had been staged in anticipation of structural collapse rather than combat, and she saw what no one else had time to notice in the middle of returning fire and shouted repositioning. A pair of breaching charges sat clipped to the bulkhead just inside the ramp, the kind meant to punch doors and walls, not clear courtyards, their placement obvious only because Grace spent her life looking at what people brought along just in case.

She didn't ask.

Grace left the crate exactly where it was and sprinted for the ramp, boots skidding on loose stone as rounds cracked and trexium fire streaked overhead, and grabbed the charges in one smooth motion, already moving again before anyone had time to process what she was doing. Someone shouted her name, sharp with alarm rather than command, and she felt the weight of the charges settle into her hands as she ran back into the open, heart hammering hard enough that it crowded out everything else.

The courtyard was a mess of movement and noise now, War Born spread thin and raiders pouring in from the edges, and Grace cut across it at a dead run, angling for the collapsed fountain structure at the center where debris had piled high enough to block clean lines of fire but low enough that people were still trying to use it as cover. She slid to a stop on one knee and slammed the first charge into place against the fractured stone, fingers flying as she armed it with movements that had nothing to do with bravery and everything to do with familiarity.

"This is going to be loud," she called, not shouting so much as projecting, her voice cutting through the chaos because she didn't bother trying to sound calm. "Move or don't, but don't be here."

Grace placed the second charge lower, offsetting it just enough to shape the blast instead of letting it throw debris in every direction, and thumbed the detonator as she threw herself backward, rolling hard across the stone and coming up behind the crate just as the world tore itself open.

The explosion was controlled only in the sense that it did exactly what Grace intended it to do, the fountain structure collapsing inward and outward at the same time, stone and metal blasting across the center of the courtyard in a violent wave that shredded the raiders pushing through and sent the rest scrambling for cover that no longer existed. The blast punched the air out of Grace's lungs and rattled the crate hard enough to make the stabilizers scream, and she was on it instantly, hands braced as she forced the systems to ride out the shock instead of fighting it.

Where there had been open ground and bad angles, there was now a cratered barrier of debris that broke sightlines and created hard cover. The raiders' momentum shattered as completely as the fountain had been. War Born surged into the space Grace had carved for them, formations snapping back into something disciplined and deadly as they took advantage of the sudden advantage, and the fight turned so quickly it felt unreal.

Grace stayed with the crate, riding the aftershocks as the stabilizers settled back into a manageable rhythm, her hands moving automatically to keep the trexium calm while the sounds of combat moved away from the courtyard and deeper into the stronghold. Only when the noise thinned and the echoes stretched out again did she realize how quiet it had become around her.

Varek approached her in the ensuing quiet and looked at her quizzically, a half smile visible behind his visor.

"At least you warned me before the explosion this time."

Chapter 8 – A Taste of Grass

The mess hall on the Vanguard side of the stronghold didn't smell like the one she remembered, not exactly, but there was enough overlap in the heat and the recycled air and the faint undercurrent of something burned that it tugged at a place in her chest she hadn't realized had been holding tension for a long time. She paused just inside the entry, hand still resting on the strap of her pack, and let the noise wash over her before she stepped fully in.

It had been years since she'd eaten here without a schedule pressing down on her, without someone waiting on her to finish so they could tell her where to be next. Training had a way of sanding the edges off time, stretching weeks into blurs and compressing months into a sequence of drills, evaluations, deployments that weren't quite deployments, and deployments that were. She'd learned how to move with armor on her shoulders before she'd ever been issued her own, learned how to think while running and fixing and shooting and not doing any of those things quite the way the instructors wanted, but well enough that no one could argue with the results.

She hadn't planned on becoming Vanguard.

She'd argued about it, quietly and then not so quietly, and she'd lost every time, worn down by a combination of necessity and Varek's particular talent for stating things as if they were already decided. Engineering knowledge didn't stay in the hangar anymore, he'd told her, not in the kinds of fights they were fighting now, and she could either keep pretending she belonged somewhere else or accept that the battlefield had already made room for her whether she liked it or not.

Grace stepped into the line and took a tray, the motion familiar enough that it settled her nerves without her having to think about it. She grabbed whatever was closest to edible and moved toward an open stretch of table, already rehearsing how she'd explain, again, why she wasn't interested in whatever protein substitute they'd decided to pretend was meat today.

Someone slid into the bench across from her with a clatter and an exaggerated sigh.

"Okay," the man said, leaning back and grinning like he'd just won something. "You have *got* to tell me about this drink."

Grace blinked, then laughed. "You heard about that already?"

"Heard about it?" He scoffed. "You've mentioned it four times since you sat down. Green. Hot. Bitter. Foam? I don't even know what part of that is supposed to be appealing."

"It's not foam," Grace said, poking at her food absently. "It's just... textured. And it's not bitter if you do it right."

The woman beside him snorted. "You're describing grass."

Grace rolled her eyes. "I am not. It's matcha. They served it when we were on diplomatic guard rotation in the south basin. Actual ceramic cups. Someone explained the ritual and everything."

"That somehow makes it worse," the man said. "You're telling me you stood there, armed to the teeth, while someone walked you through the *proper* way to drink warm leaf powder."

"It's not leaf powder," Grace said, then stopped and reconsidered. "Okay, it's leaf powder, but that's not the point."

The woman leaned across the table, eyes bright. "You like drinking grass."

"I do not."

"You do," the man said decisively. "You're smiling when you talk about it. That's how we know."

Grace opened her mouth to argue and then shut it again when she realized he was right, the corner of her mouth already lifting despite herself. "That's not—"

"Grassie," the woman said, nodding like she'd solved something important.

There was a beat of silence, just long enough for the sound to land and settle.

Grace stared at them, then down at her tray, then back up again. "No."

"Oh, it's absolutely too late," the man said, delighted. "You said it yourself. Leaf powder. Warm. Ritualized. Grass."

She groaned and leaned back, scrubbing a hand over her face. "I hate you."

"You're welcome," the woman replied cheerfully.

Grace shook her head, but the name stuck immediately, sliding into place with the kind of inevitability she'd learned not to fight anymore. Some things just happened when enough people decided they did.

She was halfway through her meal when a familiar voice cut through the noise like it had never left.

"Well, I'll be damned."

Grace looked up and felt something in her chest loosen all at once.

Dabs stood at the end of the table, looking older and broader than she remembered, grease still ingrained in his hands in a way that suggested some things hadn't changed at all. Bow was just behind him, expression calm and steady as ever, eyes already taking her in and cataloging the differences she hadn't bothered to think about.

Grace was on her feet before she realized she'd moved, the bench scraping loudly as she stepped around the table and into Dabs's arms, the impact knocking the breath out of both of them.

"You disappeared," Dabs said into her shoulder, laughing. "Just—poof. Vanguard stole you."

"You make it sound like a crime," Grace said, pulling back enough to look at him. "And I didn't disappear. I just got... occupied."

Dabs pulled back just enough to get a better look at her, hands still gripping her shoulders like he wasn't convinced she was solid yet. His grin shifted, settling into something quieter.

"Occupied," he said, nodding once. "That explains the haircut."

Grace snorted. "That was a mistake with clippers and a bad mirror."

Bow stepped in beside them without comment, the three of them forming a familiar, slightly awkward triangle that hadn't changed as much as Grace had expected. He looked her over the way he always did, eyes taking in details instead of the whole, then gave a small nod.

"You're standing different," he said.

She rolled her shoulders, aware of it only because he'd named it. "Armor drills."

"Makes sense."

They claimed a stretch of table without discussion, Dabs already pulling food toward them like it might disappear if he didn't guard it, Bow sitting with his back to the wall out of habit. Conversation came in sideways, never landing where Grace expected it to, jumping from people she half remembered to places she'd never been, stories overlapping and interrupting each other in the way that meant no one was keeping score.

Dabs talked about a pump assembly that had blown its seals three times in one week, hands moving as much as his mouth, each retelling growing more dramatic until Grace leaned across the table and flicked a crumb at him.

"You didn't almost die," she said. "You got wet."

"Wet," he repeated. "In freezing runoff, Grassie."

She paused, fork halfway to her mouth. "Don't."

Bow's mouth twitched. "Too late."

The name circled the table once, then again, picked up and tossed back with growing confidence, and Grace let it happen, pushing at it half-heartedly before giving up when she realized she was smiling again.

They drifted out of the hall later, when the noise thinned and the air grew stale, following the sound of voices toward the maintenance yard where someone had coaxed a fire into life between welded scrap plates. The flames burned low and steady, throwing uneven light across familiar faces, and Grace settled back against a crate with her boots stretched toward the heat, the chill of the night finally reaching her now that she'd stopped moving.

Someone dealt cards. Someone argued about rules. Dabs lost immediately and loudly, accusing the deck of being cursed while Bow quietly gathered the pot without comment. Grace watched the sparks rise into the dark, listened to the cadence of laughter and argument, and felt something inside her loosen with each passing minute.

At one point, someone passed her a dented tin cup. She took a sip, considered it, then nodded.

"Acceptable," she said. "Still not matcha."

Groans followed.

"You're never living that down," Dabs said.

"Good," she replied. "It'll keep you all humble."

The fire burned lower as the night deepened, conversation fading into smaller clusters, people leaning closer without realizing it. Grace tilted her head back to look at the sliver of sky visible above the yard, stars faint but stubborn against the glow, and for a moment let herself be exactly where she was, no one asking her to fix anything, no one waiting on her to decide what came next.

Her wrist chimed softly, the sound almost lost in the crackle of the fire.

Grace glanced down, thumb hovering over the display longer than it needed to, then turned her wrist just enough to dim it again without opening the message. Whatever expression crossed her face was brief, gone before anyone could pin it down, and she let the conversation around her keep going for another few seconds before she leaned forward and pushed herself to her feet.

"Walk with me," she said, already slinging her pack back over her shoulder.

Dabs blinked. "That's ominous."

"It's not ominous," Grace said. "It's... timely."

Bow was on his feet before Dabs finished talking, falling into step beside her without comment, the three of them peeling away from the fire and leaving the noise and warmth behind. The maintenance yard faded quickly, the light dropping off as they moved into the corridors that cut through the stronghold's quieter sections, footsteps echoing differently now that the night cycle had settled in and most people had found places to be still.

Dabs filled the silence out of habit, speculating wildly about what she was dragging them off for and whether it involved paperwork or explosions, while Grace kept walking and let him talk, nodding occasionally without offering any clarification. Bow watched her instead, eyes tracking the set of her shoulders, the way her pace never quite faltered even when the corridors narrowed or the lighting dipped lower than it should have.

Her quarters sat at the far end of a residential run that hadn't quite decided what it was yet, the walls still bare enough that the space felt borrowed rather than owned. Grace stopped just inside the doorway and stepped aside, letting them enter ahead of her.

Dabs took two steps in and stopped.

"Oh," he said, the word landing flat and quiet in a way that surprised all three of them.

Bow didn't speak at all. He just stood there, gaze fixed on the armor waiting on its stand near the far wall, the dark plating catching the overhead light in muted reflections that made it look heavier than it probably was. It wasn't pristine. The edges were worn, the surface marked by use and repair, the kind of wear that came from being trusted and taken back into the field again and again.

Grace stayed by the door for a moment longer, watching them take it in, then closed it softly behind her.

"Don't touch it," Dabs said, still staring. "I mean—unless you're supposed to. Are you supposed to?"

Grace shrugged one shoulder. "Eventually."

Bow turned then, looking at her with an expression that held more questions than words. "When?"

"Today," she said simply.

Dabs let out a low whistle. "So this is it."

Grace crossed the room and stopped in front of the armor, close enough now that she could see the small scratches along the edges, the places where someone else's habits had shaped the metal before it had been reissued. She reached out, then stopped herself, letting her hand hover just short of the plating as if she were still deciding whether it was real.

Bow moved closer, standing just behind her shoulder. "You didn't say anything."

"I didn't know how," Grace said. "And then I didn't have time."

He nodded once, as if that explained more than it should have.

She turned away from the armor and crossed to the narrow shelf along the wall, fingers brushing past tools and folded clothes until they found the strip of yellow cloth she'd kept through moves and rotations and long stretches where she'd forgotten it was even hers. The fabric was worn soft, edges frayed just enough to show it had been handled more than admired, carried through places that hadn't cared about color or memory.

Grace held it up against the armor, the yellow breaking the dark lines, bright and stubborn and unmistakably out of place, and for the first time let herself imagine what it would look like once it wasn't standing still. Images of lightning streaking across the battlefield filled her mind's eye.

Dabs laughed softly, the sound full and a little rough. "Figures."

Bow smiled, small and quiet, and didn't say anything at all.

Grace lowered the cloth and looked at the armor again, then back at the two of them, feeling something settle into place that had been shifting for a long time.

"Stay a bit," she said, almost as a question. "Before I put it on."

Dabs nodded immediately. "Yeah."

Bow nodded in his quiet way

Grassie Smiled.

Chapter 9 – Before the Drop

The war room always ran hot, no matter how recently it had been cleared or how many times the filters had been cycled, the heat bleeding steadily off the old shield rigs tucked into the corners as if they resented being idle. Grassie felt it through the soles of her boots before she registered it anywhere else, the vibration threading up through cracked tile and into her legs, the hum settling into a rhythm she cataloged without effort, the way other people noticed changes in light or sound.

Dust drifted through the overhead fixtures in slow, careless curls, catching on armor edges and gloved hands, on the battered central table that had been dragged through three strongholds and never fully repaired. One corner still bore old tally marks scratched into the surface, shallow enough to be ignored until you knew to look for them, and Grassie's eyes flicked to them out of habit before sliding back to what mattered, because some patterns stayed useful even when you didn't know who had started them.

She stood to Daryas' left, arms folded loosely, one foot tapping against the floor in a quiet, steady rhythm that kept her grounded when too many variables competed for attention. She wasn't looking at the map yet. She was watching Daryas, because that was what she had learned to do when the room tightened and decisions had to be clean.

The armor fit Daryas now. Not the way it had at the beginning, when every movement had been deliberate and checked twice, but the way it did once someone stopped thinking about it as equipment and started treating it like an extension of their body. The scuffs along Daryas' thigh plates weren't random anymore; they followed patterns, told stories about how she turned under pressure, how she planted herself when others hesitated, how she moved through doorways without ever breaking stride. Grassie remembered the first time she'd seen her—sharp edges, too much fury and sadness held too tight—and the difference now wasn't softer so much as steadier, grief turned into something useful.

Commander Hartwell stood at the front of the room, datapad loose in his gloved hand, posture rigid in the way officers adopted when the margin for error had already been spent.

"Delta-Echo-Five deployed two days ago," Hartwell said, his voice cutting clean through the room's low hum. "Standard rotation. Minimal scavenger risk expected. Then comms cut. Scouts confirm survivors pinned in the main depot block. Civilian assets trapped inside. Raiders have fortified the outer yards."

He tapped the pad once, flicking up an overhead scan of the depot—half the perimeter fencing collapsed inward, dark scoring along the main road, the supply yards gutted and left to rot.

Grassie's attention shifted to the image automatically, eyes tracing blind angles and choke points, noting where collapsed fencing would funnel movement and where scoring suggested recent activity rather than simple decay.

"We have a window," Hartwell said. "We move now, we get them out. If we wait—" he paused, gaze sweeping across them, "—we lose everyone."

Smokey's voice slid in from the back, casual but sharp.

"What's the plan for insert? Flyers are still grounded after Zeta-Four, right?"

Hartwell's jaw tightened, but he nodded.

"No Vanguard flyers. Lost too many packs during the evacuation collapse. Ground-to-air sabotage."

He adjusted the pad. "That leaves rigs to the perimeter. One pass. No fallback."

Grassie felt the room tighten as the words landed, the same way systems tightened under load, everyone shifting weight without meaning to as they pictured the same thing and didn't bother pretending otherwise.

Daryas shifted her stance slightly, a small movement that Grassie registered more than saw, and Hartwell dropped the next words like they were nothing special.

"Skyhammer maneuver."

Cab froze for a half-second, her gloved hands tightening on the edge of the table.

Grassie let out a slow breath through her nose, almost a sigh.

Daryas watched Hartwell without blinking.

"No one's done a Skyhammer landing in the field in years," Cab said, voice a little too loud before she caught herself, swallowing hard. "We've all done the training, but—"

"It's too dangerous unless there's no other choice," Smokey finished for her, the usual edge of humor in his voice blunted to something heavier.

Hartwell simply nodded once. "There's no other choice."

Rich shifted his stance near the wall, the faint grind of boot against stone the only sign of movement.

"You realize if we don't land this perfectly," Grassie said, voice low and even, "we become the crater."

Daryas cut in without hesitation, her voice steady. "Then we don't do it wrong."

The room absorbed that in silence for a breath, the old lighting buzzing louder overhead as if it was trying to compete with the thought.

Hartwell flicked the pad again, the depot's broken map reappearing.

"Targets inside are pinned under the admin block," he said. "Civilians mixed with wounded. Raider forces are controlling the west approach and the inner loading yards. East side partially collapsed—unstable. Watch for falling debris."

He tapped one corner of the map, highlighting a small cluster of signature pings.

"Intel shows at least thirty combatants still moving inside the walls. Maybe more."

Cab shifted again, fidgeting with the chinstrap of her helmet.

Hartwell's tone didn't change. "Expect dirty. Expect traps."

He tapped one final marker onto the overhead.

"And expect Kallan Brigg."

The name slid across the room like a dropped knife.

Smokey whistled low between his teeth. "Kallan 'One Shot' Brigg?"

Rich's visor tipped slightly in confusion. "Who?"

Daryas turned her head slightly toward him, catching a glint of light across the unbroken surface of his helmet.

"You don't know Brigg?" Smokey asked, half grinning like he couldn't believe it. "Old raider captain. Used to run hit-and-fades against Coalition scout posts. Supposedly took out a base commander with one shot from a half-broken hunting rifle during the fall at Grent's Crossing. That was without optics."

"Heard he once took down a supply rig with a pistol from a moving crawler," Grassie added, voice dry as desert stone.

"Probably half lies," Daryas said, but that wasn't the half that concerned her. It was the rest that were truths.

Even if the stories were inflated, they didn't make him less dangerous, especially cornered.

Hartwell folded the pad closed with a snap.

"You have twenty minutes. Get ready."

The loading bay rattled with noise.

Engines coughed and roared in cycles as crews hauled supply crates and landing gear into battered rigs lined along the perimeter gates. The air smelled of hot oil, charged battery packs, and the metallic tang of weapon lubricant baking under the midday heat.

Grassie adjusted the strap across her chest as she dropped down the stairs from the war room, boots hitting cracked concrete hard enough to feel it through her shins. The squad fell into place without needing to be called—Rich ghosting along the edges of the group, head tilted slightly as he cross-checked the loadouts without removing his helmet; Cab jogging to catch up, helmet tucked under her arm, armor shifting loose where she hadn't tightened the straps properly yet; Smokey already waiting by the closest rig, leaning back against the cargo ramp like he had all the time in the world.

"You really believe that Brigg crap?" Rich asked over the squad comms, voice filtered into its usual low growl through his visor.

Smokey grinned, flipping his rifle upright with a lazy twist. "Guy's a walking cautionary tale. You screw around long enough, someone remembers your best shot and forgets the six times you missed."

"Sounds like someone's jealous," Cab muttered, fumbling with the clasp on her thigh rig.

Smokey slid his gaze sideways, all mock offense. "Jealous? Please. My worst day's cleaner than Brigg's best."

"Except for that time you got smoked in training," Grassie said mildly, stepping up to check the charge cells lining the side of their packs.

"Different circumstances," Smokey said without missing a beat. "I was operating under extreme tactical creativity."

Grassie let a short snort out and went back to her checks, because the banter wasn't noise so much as pressure bleeding off, the squad finding their footing in the only way they ever did when the ground underneath them started to crack.

Cab's hands were shaking again.

Grassie noticed. So did Daryas.

Daryas stepped in without making a show of it, tapping two fingers lightly against the side of Cab's arm as she passed.

"You're ready," she said, voice low enough not to carry beyond them.

Cab drew a sharp breath in, nodded once, and tucked her chin down to check her boots like it was just another checklist item.

The rig doors ahead were swinging open now, the massive lift arms creaking under the strain. The carrier itself crouched low against the deck, its surface scarred with old blast marks and patch jobs welded into ugly plates.

No Vanguard flyers. No clean drops. Just steel and speed and bad odds.

Grassie caught the shift in Daryas's posture before she consciously registered why it mattered, the subtle tightening across her shoulders telegraphing readiness the same way a system change telegraphed load before numbers caught up. Daryas's hand moved to her rifle, drawing it in closer against her chest as she glanced across the yard toward the airship's boarding ramp, and Grassie followed the line of sight without thinking, already cataloging the layout around the rig holds.

The burn packs were laid out in neat rows near the ramp, small and brutally utilitarian, each one a single chance disguised as equipment, and Grassie moved through them on instinct, checking seals and straps as she went. She picked up two without comment, tossing one to Cab, who bobbled it against her chest before catching it properly, her jaw tightening as she keyed the harness home.

Smokey caught Daryas's eye across the movement of crews strapping down med kits and emergency harnesses on other rigs bound for other problems, and Grassie saw the exchange without intruding on it, the brief lift of his brow, the smirk that never quite reached his mouth. Daryas stepped closer as the squad gathered at the ramp, her shoulder pressing lightly into Smokey's through the armor, and Grassie registered the contact the same way she registered a tightened strap or a checked seal—brief, grounding, functional.

The rig engines deepened into a steady growl, deck plates vibrating under Grassie's boots as the main power feeds kicked through, and she shifted her weight to accommodate it without breaking stride. Cab finished locking her harness, knuckles white around the straps, and Grassie reached out to give them one last tug, not because Cab needed it, but because the ritual mattered.

Rich murmured low confirmations over the comms as he ran another systems check from memory, his voice steady and precise, and Grassie grunted responses automatically, tracking the cadence more than the words, because the rhythm told her everything she needed to know.

Daryas keyed the squad channel.

"Final checks. Strap in tight. On my mark, we go."

The rig captain shouted boarding clearance across the open bay, his voice crackling over the rough speaker, and Grassie felt the horizon shiver under the heat haze beyond the gates, Delta-Echo-Five's broken outline crouched low against the earth like a problem that had decided not to solve itself.

Daryas moved to the ramp first, boots thudding solidly against steel, and Grassie stepped in beside her without pause, slotting to her left as naturally as breathing. Smokey fell in at Daryas's right, Cab and Rich tightening the formation behind them until the space between bodies disappeared and movement became shared responsibility.

They sealed the hatch behind them with the low grind of old hydraulics, and inside the carrier the light dropped to emergency red, casting hard angles across armor and faces, sharpening edges Grassie already knew by heart. She rolled her shoulders once, feeling the pack straps creak against her armor as she settled into the stance she used when gravity was about to become an argument.

Skyhammer wasn't a word in her head so much as a checklist she'd already completed.

One drop.

One chance.

She curled her hand into a loose fist against her thigh and let the hum of the engines and the slow, heavy breath of the squad fill the space between thoughts, the silence carrying weight without needing ceremony.

No speeches. No drama. Just the kind of trust that came from knowing exactly who would be where when everything else fell away.

The rig jerked hard as the engines kicked into full thrust, the deck rattling under Grassie's boots, and the world outside blurred into light and dust and the savage promise of the drop to come.

Chapter 10 – The War Angels

The moment gravity took hold, Grassie stopped thinking in sentences. Wind tore at her armor, a raw, screaming pressure that flattened everything down to angles and velocity, and she tucked in tight, letting the burn pack carry her weight for the fraction of time it was designed to survive. The depot yard surged up beneath her in broken planes of concrete and metal, shadows snapping into focus as the distance collapsed faster than instinct wanted to believe.

She fired late.

The thrusters slammed her upright in a violent wrench that drove breath from her lungs and rattled her teeth, boots skidding across cracked paneling that barely disguised the earth underneath, and she rolled hard into cover without waiting to see if the landing had been clean. It had to be. The rest would sort itself out.

Noise arrived all at once.

Gunfire ripped through the yard in jagged bursts, trexium rounds hissing past close enough that heat licked along her armor seals, generators screaming awake somewhere to her right as ancient systems tried to decide whether this was an emergency they were meant to handle. Grassie pressed herself low behind a shattered supply crate and let the chaos resolve into patterns, muzzle flashes sketching lines across the dust, bodies moving where they shouldn't have been able to move that fast.

War Born hit the ground around her in the spread they'd practiced a hundred times, the yard reorganizing itself around their impact whether it wanted to or not. Rich landed heavy to her right, armor taking the hit like it always did, rifle already barking controlled bursts that anchored the flank before anyone thought to name it. Cab dropped wide, momentum carrying her into a rolling slide that ended in a crouch behind a scorched vehicle hull, laughter crackling once over comms before she went quiet and lethal.

Smokey came down fast and fluid on the opposite edge, his rifle snapping into place as if it had never known another job.

Daryas took the center.

Grassie didn't watch her for long. She didn't need to. The line held because it always did when Daryas was there, and Grassie trusted that the space behind her would stay solid long enough for Grassie to do her own work.

A raider broke from cover ahead, muzzle flashing wild. Grassie leaned out just enough to put two short bursts into his center mass before he finished adjusting his aim, then slid left and dropped the second man who thought the first had drawn all the fire. She stayed low and fast, not chasing kills so much as trimming options, forcing movement into narrower lanes where Rich's heavier fire could take over.

Dust thickened as explosions punched into the yard, debris raining down in sharp, ugly fragments that ricocheted off armor and crate edges, and Grassie shifted position again, letting the storm pass over her instead of trying to outrun it. She felt the yard change as they pushed, pressure pulling inward toward the depot's broken mouth, raiders scrambling for elevation and cover that stopped working the moment War Born decided to take it away from them.

They cleared the outer yard faster than she'd expected.

That was when the fight stopped being simple.

Grassie caught the shift before anyone called it out, the way raiders stopped running and started clustering, their movement tightening around something they cared about. She followed the line of it through the haze and saw the civilians huddled near the collapsed loading dock, pinned behind overturned pallets and twisted girders, raiders stacked above them on broken scaffolding and half-fallen walkways.

Daryas pivoted without hesitation, the movement clean and decisive.

She caught Daryas pivoting low behind cover, scanning fast, and then the comm snapped in her ear with the line that meant the plan had just changed.

"Secondary group located. Northeast quadrant."

Grassie answered immediately, voice clipped, because the answer needed to be simple.

"Acknowledged. Holding outer yard."

Rich's response came steady.

"Anchor left. Covering your push."

Smokey's voice followed, dry even now.

"You're gonna owe me coffee if you get yourself killed."

Rich's response came steady and immediate. "Anchor left. Covering."

Smokey's voice cut in, dry even now. "You're gonna owe me coffee if you get yourself killed."

Grassie snorted and went quiet, because Daryas was already moving toward the civilians and the rest of them needed to make sure nothing followed.

She shifted into a new lane and started trading fire across the loading ramp, picking targets that threatened to collapse the space Daryas was pushing through. Cab crashed into a fallback position with brute enthusiasm, breaking a cluster of raiders before they could stabilize, and Rich stepped forward into the gap she left behind, his bulk turning scattered return fire into noise instead of danger.

Then Grassie saw him.

He moved wrong for a raider.

Too calm. Too deliberate. Armor scavenged and reinforced, heavier than the rest, cutting through chaos like it was familiar ground. Grassie felt the tension spike in her chest before she registered the reason, the way systems reacted when load exceeded tolerance.

Brigg.

She adjusted her fire instinctively, trying to carve a path toward Smokey's position as Smokey broke from cover to intercept, but the yard buckled under her feet as raiders flooded into her lane, forcing her to hold instead of advance. She dropped three, then two more, but the distance to Smokey only grew, the fight pulling apart into pockets she couldn't cross fast enough.

Smokey went to blades when his rifle became useless at that range, moving fast and tight, dodging swings that would have flattened someone else, but Brigg fought like a collapsing wall, every hit meant to end things. Grassie fired twice at angles that should have hit and didn't, the shots chewing debris instead of flesh, and frustration burned sharp at the back of her throat.

Brigg's voice carried through the yard, clear and cruel.

"I've heard about you. Best shot in the Vanguard, they say."

Grassie shifted again, ignoring Cab's warning, trying to force an opening that refused to appear.

"Let's see how sharp that eye really is."

Smokey staggered under the blow, blood flashing bright against dust, and Grassie felt the sick, cold drop of being too far away settle into her gut. She planted her boots and emptied the rest of her magazine into the raiders hemming her in, clearing space inch by inch, but Smokey was already on his knees, Brigg looming over him with a machete drawn slow, almost ceremonial.

Then the yard split open.

Not with sound at first, but with light.

A single trexium blast cut through the haze, brighter and hotter than issue, the beam tearing a clean line across the chaos and punching through Brigg's temple before the rest of his body caught up with the idea of being dead. He collapsed in a heap, machete clattering uselessly against the ground.

The yard stuttered.

Grassie froze for half a heartbeat, just long enough to register Smokey still breathing, still upright, still alive, and then she moved again, because the fight wasn't over just because its center had fallen out. She took down the raider reaching for Smokey, then the one trying to drag Brigg's body back, then shifted her fire outward to keep the yard from re-forming.

Only when the noise thinned and the survivors scattered did she let herself look for Daryas.

She found her standing near the depot wall, rifle lowered but still ready, armor scorched and cracked where the landing had bitten deepest, chest heaving as the last of the old core's power bled out. Grassie didn't need to see the diagnostics to know what Daryas had done. She'd felt it in the heat of the shot, in the way the blast had burned cleaner than it should have.

Smokey slumped to his knees, one hand pressed to his face, blood seeping through his fingers but alive, and Grassie moved without thinking, dragging him back into cover while Cab covered them with a stream of suppressing fire that discouraged curiosity.

When the smoke finally lifted, Delta-Echo-Five loomed behind them in the dying light, broken walls breathing out lazy arcs of smoke like the last breath of something too stubborn to fall cleanly. Civilians clustered near the medical rigs, shaken and bleeding but alive, eyes flicking toward the squad and away again as if they weren't sure what to call what they'd just seen.

Grassie wiped dust and blood from her faceplate with the back of her glove and slid into formation near the rear ramp, helmet tucked under her arm, body finally registering the ache that had been waiting its turn. Rich leaned against the rig wall, rifle resting across his chest, helmet still sealed. Cab lowered herself onto a crate, nose split and bleeding, helmet dangling from tired fingers. Smokey stood in the shadow of the rig frame, stitches already biting into raw skin, one eye swollen shut, the other tracking Daryas with something unspoken and steady.

Commander Hartwell crossed the yard toward them, boots crunching over debris, armor still dusted white with ash. He stopped a few paces out and studied them for a long moment, the silence heavier than any reprimand.

"You pulled them out," he said at last. "All of them."

His gaze flicked toward the civilians, then back.

"You hit that yard like an airstrike. Fast. Brutal." He shook his head once. "Like an air strike from heaven."

The words landed harder than Grassie expected, not because they were praise, but because they named something she'd felt happening without ever putting words to it.

Hartwell turned away and started shouting orders to the med teams, leaving the squad standing in the quiet that followed.

Grassie looked around the yard at the smoke, the survivors, the way the world had reorganized itself around them, and felt the shift settle fully into place. Whatever they had been before, it wasn't enough anymore.

They weren't just holding the line.

They were changing it.

And when the dust finally settled, the name that followed them felt inevitable.

They were the War Angels.

Between the Flames

The fire had burned down to coals by the time Grassie stopped.

She hadn't planned to end it there necessarily. The last sentence just came out slower than the rest, and then there wasn't anything after it that didn't feel like it would be pushing. She nudged a coal back toward the center with the edge of her boot and let the quiet settle.

Miner sat across from her, mug braced between both hands. He didn't look at her when she finished. He watched the coals, the way he always did when he was listening for what came next instead of what had already been said.

The wind shifted, smoke drifting low and stinging the back of Grassie's throat. She turned her head slightly and spat to the side, then leaned back against the stone.

Cab broke the silence by rolling a pebble between her fingers and flicking it into the coals. It sparked once and disappeared.

"That part with the ridge," she said. "You skipped it."

Grassie didn't look up. "It wasn't important to the story."

Cab shook her head. "Maybe, but you still almost went off."

Grassie adjusted the strap on her boot as she rolled, leather creaking. "My footing slipped."

Miner glanced up at that, just briefly, then back to the fire.

Daryas leaned forward, forearms on her knees, gaze steady on the coals. "Smokey grabbed you."

Grassie paused. Then nodded once. "Yeah."

That was all she said, and it was enough to change the shape of the silence that surrounded all of them after the syllable.

Rich shifted closer to the fire, boots scraping stone. He stopped there, arms folded, helmet still resting where he'd set it earlier.

"He yelled at you," Rich said.

Grassie huffed a short breath. "He always yelled."

"He told you to stop arguing with the stabilizer," Cab added.

Grassie's mouth twitched despite herself. "It was arguing back."

Miner let out a low sound that might've been a laugh, then tipped his mug and took a careful drink. The metal clinked softly when he set it back down.

The space beside the fire stayed empty. The stone there still held heat, like someone had been sitting there recently and just hadn't come back yet.

Grassie picked at the edge of her boot strap with the tip of her knife, not cutting, just tracing the worn seam. "I told it how I remember it."

Daryas nodded. "We know."

Cab stared into the coals. "I wonder if that's how he'd remember it."

Grassie glanced at her. "Maybe."

Cab shrugged. "I wish he were here. He could tell his story. I bet it was interesting enough."

Daryas straightened then, not sharply, just enough to pull the circle back into shape. She reached forward and added another piece of wood to the coals, careful with it, like she didn't want the fire to jump.

"I'm willing to bet," Daryas said. Her voice was even. Not soft. Not hard. "That we could still get his story."

Grassie looked at her. "He's not here."

"I know," Daryas said. "But we are. And I bet we all have enough pieces to do him justice."

Miner's mouth curved slightly at that. He shifted his weight against the stone and waited.

Rich stepped closer, closing the gap without comment.

Cab sighed and rubbed a hand over her face. "He'd already be interrupting."

Daryas's mouth twitched. "Yes. Yes, he would."

They all looked around the circle once, then back at Daryas. "Go on then. You're the only one who would know the beginning."

Daryas leaned back against the rock, knife resting flat across her boot. She felt the heat on her shins, the ache in her shoulders, the cold pressing in around the fire.

"If I miss something," she said.

Cab answered immediately. "We'll tell you."

Daryas nodded. "Good."

The fire crackled low between them as Daryas spoke again, and the story moved forward—not cleanly, not in order, but the way it always had when they were all still alive to argue about it.

www.ingramcontent.com/pod-product-compliance
Lightning Source LLC
Chambersburg PA
CBHW070643130626
46555CB00006B/2674